You've Got To Believe Me

JUDITH ST GEORGE

YOU'VE GOT TO BELIEVE ME

Methuen

First published in the United States 1982
by G. P. Putnam's Sons, New York
under the title *Do You See What I See?*
First published in Great Britain in 1988
by Methuen Children's Books Ltd
11 New Fetter Lane, London EC4P 4EE
Copyright © 1982 Judith St George
Printed in Great Britain by
Redwood Burn Limited,
Trowbridge, Wiltshire.

British Library Cataloguing in Publication Data

St. George, Judith
[Do you see what I see?]   You've got to believe me.
I. [Do you see what I see?]   II. Title
813'.54[J]   PZ7

ISBN 0-416-05162-6

To Marge and Paul

You've Got To Believe Me

1

*T*here he was again, way across the salt marsh down by the sluice bridge, the red fox Matt had seen twice before. His full winter coat shone like copper and his bushy tail was as thick as a muff. Matt raised an imaginary rifle to his shoulder, lined up the fox in his sights and blasted away. POW! POW! The fox, unaware of Matt's presence or the fictitious volley, gave a flick of his white-tipped tail and disappeared behind the dead stalks of the wintry brown marsh grass.

Matt leaned back against the huge solitary boulder he called Black Rock. Actually, it wasn't a rock at all, but a gray, lichen-covered boulder that a glacier had deposited here on the edge of the marsh thousands of years ago. Now Matt swung the rifle toward the north end of the marsh where Tebby was racing through the shallow tidal creeks. The phantom rifle seemed so real to him he could almost feel the weight of its butt fit into his shoulder. He picked Tebby up in his sights, a big black Labrador retriever, as rambunctious as a puppy, although she was more than four years old. Now all Matt could see of her was the top of her ebony head above the rustling marsh grass.

Suddenly a pair of mallard ducks exploded into the air, followed by a barking and triumphant Tebby. Matt waited until the ducks had steadied their course, then took aim at the glossy green head of the male. POW! Then the female's brown head. POW! In his mind's eye, he saw them plummet from the sky.

"Fetch!" he yelled at Tebby, who merely turned her head at the sound of his voice before plunging back into the shallow, cold March water. Some retriever she was. Well, next year, when Matt got a hunting permit for real, he'd train her properly.

Matt slumped tiredly against Black Rock and pulled up the collar of his down vest. Wind, wind, wind. Didn't the wind ever stop blowing? It wasn't even very cold out, only about 45 degrees, but that everlasting sea wind chilled him to the marrow. He ran his fingers through his thick brown hair. Not only did the damp wind freeze his gut, but it kept his hair so curly he had it cut every few weeks just to look decent, even though it did make his already big ears seem to stick out more.

Matt sighed as he watched Tebby head for the far side of the marsh. Maybe she was onto the trail of that red fox. If only he had a real rifle. He lined Tebby up and slowly scanned the marsh. Nimicut Salt Marsh was small, only about ten acres, and now in March, with its brown grasses stiff and jagged, it resembled a giant lumpy pancake. Narrow tidal creeks fingered through the marsh over salt ice crusts left from previous tides. Drab pitch pines and stunted scrub oaks surrounded the marsh on three sides, with the sand dunes of the Cape Cod outer beach ribboning its eastern boundary. Beyond the dunes, the bleak Atlantic Ocean stretched endlessly toward Spain. Now, at 6:30 in the morning, a salmon-red sun edged its way over a pewter sea.

Hey, hold it. Matt picked up a flicker of movement just beyond his range, high and to the north. It was something foreign, out of sync with the rustling grasses and whistling wind, a person, a man, up on the deck of the only house visible from the marsh, a little gray shingled cottage about 400 yards away set high up on a bluff. The cottage, which overlooked the marsh to the south and the ocean to the east, had been empty ever since Matt had started walking Tebby here a month ago. But it wasn't empty now.

Matt shaded his eyes to see better. A man was up there, all right. Now he was moving around to the south deck, kneeling at the sliding door as if to pick the lock. It was a break-in.

Break-ins were a problem here on Cape Cod. Empty summer cottages were broken into and vandalized all the time. When Matt and his mother and brother Bucky had arrived in January to live in the house Mom's parents had left her, they'd found a disaster—broken furniture and smashed mirrors, with empty beer cans, rotting food, cigarette and joint butts all over the place. Just thinking about it started Matt's blood boiling. If he ever got his hands on whoever had done it, he'd . . . he'd make them pay, that's what. And maybe that man up there on the deck had been involved.

"Sst. Tebby, sst." Matt whistled softly to get Tebby's attention, but she was on the far side of the marsh pawing at something in the water that Matt couldn't see, and he didn't dare whistle louder for fear the man on the deck would hear him and take off. Matt would just have to go for help and hope that Tebby would follow.

Mrs. Shreve's house was the nearest, about a quarter of a mile away. Matt tried to pace himself as he started running, but by the time he'd gone 100 yards or so, he was already panting and his heart was racing. This stinking mononucleosis. He'd had mono for weeks now and it had kept him feeling lousy. He'd missed more school than he'd attended, and worse, he couldn't do anything without getting exhausted. Here he was, seventeen years old, almost six feet tall, weighing in at 155, taking a nap every day, if you could believe that, and now that he was about to nab some punk breaking into a house, he could hardly run. He took long, deep breaths to fill his lungs but the damp, clammy air did nothing to revive him. What he wouldn't give right now for good old mile-high mountain air.

Effort that it was, Matt kept going. And then he heard the tap of Tebby's nails on the macadam behind him. Good. Tebby belonged to Mrs. Shreve and was in Matt's charge and the last thing he needed right now was for something to happen to Tebby. They passed a few weathered gray-shingled cottages tucked behind low bayberry shrubs and pitch pines, but they were all empty, with their windows boarded up like eyelids closed, and their phones disconnected until summer. Sometimes it seemed as if Matt's family and Mrs. Shreve were the only idiots crazy enough to live on Cape Cod out of season.

"Mrs. Shreve! Mrs. Shreve! It's me, Matt Runyon. Let me in." He knew it would take her a long time to answer his knock. Mrs. Shreve had broken her ankle last month and had to use a walker that she hadn't quite mastered. It was the reason she had hired Matt to walk Tebby in the first place.

Finally the door opened. Mrs. Shreve wavered precariously on her walker as Tebby rushed past her into the narrow hall.

"Someone's breaking into that house up on the hill overlooking the marsh. I gotta call the police." Matt was breathless.

One of Mrs. Shreve's eyebrows went up and one went down in that quizzical way she had. "Bluff Cottage? That's been for sale ever since the Crowthers moved to Florida and . . ."

"What's the police number?" Matt interrupted.

"It's 275-3000, though I daresay Constable Hulse isn't there. His wife's been feeling poorly and he . . ."

Matt was already describing to the police what he had seen. He hung up and headed for the front door.

"Where are you going?" Mrs. Shreve demanded.

Where did she think he was going? "Up to the house. I want to be there when they arrest that turkey."

Mrs. Shreve pursed her lips but didn't say anything the way Mom would have, like Matt might miss his school bus, or that he might be putting himself in danger, or that it wasn't any of his business. When Mrs. Shreve voiced her opinions, they were pretty strong, but luckily, she usually kept them to herself. Although her carroty red hair had now faded to gray, she still had a redhead's freckles and lashless blue eyes and , Matt thought privately, a redhead's crisp gingersnap personality, too. But for now, she said nothing.

Matt pulled the door shut behind him, grabbed his bike and pushed off. It was all uphill to Bluff Cottage, which meant he would have to take it easy to be sure of getting there in one piece. This was the most exciting thing that had happened since he had moved to East Ted-ham, and there was no way he was going to miss out on it. As for school, the only person who would even notice he wasn't there would be the attendance secretary.

2

Matt propped his bicycle against a scraggly pine tree, then leaned against it himself. It wasn't much of a ride from Mrs. Shreve's up the hill here to Bluff Cottage, but he'd had to pedal against the wind the whole way and he was wheezing. As soon as he was breathing easier, he crouched behind a sprawling sharp-needled juniper shrub that edged the property and peered out. Right away he saw a late model Cadillac with Arizona plates parked in the driveway and a woman sitting in the front passenger seat. So there were two of them working this scam. If only the police would hurry up and get here.

As Matt shifted into a better viewing position, it began to dawn on him that the rear of the Cadillac was filled with suitcases and garment bags. And the woman in the front seat was leaning back against the headrest casually smoking a cigarette. Too casually. Matt thoughtfully rubbed his thumbnail along the narrow separation between his two front teeth. If this was a break-in, it was a pretty strange one.

Raarrff . . . raarrff . . .

Startled, Matt turned to see Tebby come barreling up

the road toward him. She must have gotten out and followed him. The woman in the car turned too.

"Hello, who's there?" She rolled down her window and looked over toward the juniper bushes.

There was no way out of it. With Tebby following, Matt reluctantly came out from behind the shrubbery and started across the front yard. As he approached the parked car, he had to shade his eyes against the glare of the sun that had already risen over the flat gray slate of the ocean to the east.

"Hi." He tried to sound nonchalant. "Can I help you?"

The woman, wearing smoked glasses and a scarf over her hair, sat as low in the car as a child. "I wish you could. " She sounded annoyed. "The realtor sent us the wrong key and we're locked out. My husband is trying to find an open door or window so we can get in."

Terrific. Any minute the police were going to come tearing up the road with their sirens wailing to arrest some guy who was locked out of his own house. Still, Matt didn't see the point in saying anything. If the police were as incompetent as Mrs. Shreve implied, maybe they wouldn't even show up.

"You're from Arizona?" he asked, rubbing his arms to warm them.

"Phoenix." The woman stubbed out her cigarette in the car ashtray and pulled out another. As she lit up, Matt noticed she wore a beautiful diamond wristwatch and ornate rings on almost every finger. Her hands were so small, the heavy jewelry looked ridiculous, especially on her right hand where part of her middle finger was missing. Matt wondered if she'd been born that way or if she'd had an accident.

"I used to live in Colorado," he volunteered, still squinting into the sun. "A little town outside of Denver . . ."

"Sidney!"

Matt jumped and so did the woman. A man stood in the now-open doorway. Obviously he'd somehow managed to get into the house. From the marsh, Matt hadn't been able to see the man's face, but by the stocky, broad-shouldered look of him, Matt was sure it was the same person. Now the man seemed furious as he slammed the front door behind him and hurried over to the car. He didn't even acknowledge Matt's presence as he climbed into the driver's side beside the woman, started up the motor and took off toward the garage. In seconds, the car had disappeared behind the house, enveloping Matt and Tebby in a burst of exhaust fumes.

Whew, that man had some temper. And it took one to know one. Matt had been born with a short fuse, or so his mother claimed. At any rate, for now this man seemed angry at his wife Sidney, or whatever her name was, and not at him and Matt would just as soon leave it that way. Which meant he had better get out of here.

But Tebby was already growling and sniffing around the shrubbery. Sure enough, a policeman, hidden by the juniper bush, was already edging up toward the house, with his police cruiser parked down the road out of sight. Matt stepped around the shrubbery.

"Ah . . ." he cleared his throat. "Hi, there . . . ah . . . I guess there's been a mistake. I mean the man I thought was trying to break into the house is renting it but doesn't have a key."

"What's your name?"

"Matthew Runyon."

"You called in the report?"

"Ah . . . yeah . . . I thought I saw a break-in from the marsh but everything's okay now."

The policeman, who wore a green windbreaker with uniform pants, Top-Siders and no hat on his half-moon of a bald head, scowled. "Wal, it won't take but a bit to check it out."

"But . . ."

The policeman had already started across the yard with Tebby trotting amiably along beside him. Matt's instinct was to take off on his bike, but he hesitated one fateful second. The policeman turned and waved his hand.

"Don't you be traveling anywheres," he ordered as he knocked on the front door. "East Tedham Borough Police," he called out.

There was no response other than the wind whining through the utility wires and the distant growl of the surf.

The knock was louder this time. "East Tedham Borough Police."

The door opened a crack.

"I'm real sorry to bother you, sir, but we got a report of an alleged break-in at this address." The policeman was all politeness.

The door opened wider, but instead of asking the officer in, the man stepped out, closing the door behind him. "What are you talking about?" he demanded.

"We got a call at 6:40 that an unauthorized person was attempting to enter these premises. Was that you, sir?"

"Of course it was me." The man's face, which was tan to begin with, flushed even darker.

"You got identification, sir?"

"I'm Charles R. Vossert, President of Hanna Industries in Phoenix." With a scowl, the man took what appeared to be a driver's license from his wallet and held it out. Putting on a pair of half glasses, the policeman took the paper and read it.

From a safe distance near the juniper bushes, Matt

studied Mr. Vossert. His hair was dark and thick, expensively styled, and though his features were oversized, with a heavy jaw, a wide mouth, a hawklike nose, he was a handsome man of about thirty-five or forty.

The policeman handed back the license. "You've rented Bluff Cottage, Mr. Vossert?"

"My wife and I rented it through O'Brien Realty in the hopes of coming to Cape Cod for a complete rest. So far we've experienced nothing but aggravation. O'Brien Realty sent us the wrong key and now at the ungodly hour of seven in the morning, you've showed up to further annoy us. What's your name, Officer?"

"Constable Lemuel Hulse. You happen to have a copy of your lease, Mr. Vossert?" Polite still, but firm.

"I have no idea where the lease is. If you want verification, just wake up that idiot realtor and let her confirm that we're the tenants. Now good day." Mr. Vossert started toward the house, then turned back. "O'Brien Realty guaranteed that we'd have no neighbors. Who reported the break-in?"

Here we go, Matt groaned inwardly. He was hoping the question wouldn't be asked, that he could just stay where he was, an innocent bystander.

But to Matt's relief, Constable Hulse fended off the question. "That's confidential, as I'm sure you can 'preciate, sir."

Unfortunately, Tebby, who had been snuffling around in the adjacent vacant lot, took that moment to wander over and nuzzle Matt's hand with her cold nose. In an attempt to disassociate himself from the whole scene, Matt fastened his attention on the flight of a distant hawk as it cruised low over the marsh beyond the house.

But Mr. Vossert must have sensed that his question had been answered because his eyes immediately shifted to Matt, taking his measure, the thin gawky length of him, the short, much too curly brown hair, the big ears, the pasty-pale complexion and the dark circled eyes from being sick with mono. "What's your name?" Vossert demanded.

It seemed to be the question of the day. "Matthew Runyon."

"Do you live near here?"

"On Old Duckhole Road." Matt was always tempted to say Old Asshole Road just to shock people. He still couldn't believe he lived on a street named Old Duckhole Road.

Vossert studied Matt another moment, then turned on his heel and stalked back into the house. When he slammed the door behind him, the flimsy rose trellises that framed the white-trim doorway trembled.

"Jest what East Tedham needs, a coupl'a satisfied tourists," Constable Hulse muttered. His mouth was a thin line as he strode past Matt without even glancing at him.

Matt could feel his own anger begin to rise and bubble like a pot simmering. What had he done? If that had been a real break-in, he would have been a big hero, that's what. As it was, everyone was treating him like a criminal. Still, what could he expect from a dump of a town like this but a dumb cop?

Matt watched Tebby follow the policeman down the hill to where his cruiser was pulled over on the grass. Look at Tebby's tail wag. Well, let it wag. She was a Cape Cod dog and that was a Cape Cod cop. Of course they'd stick together. After all, Tebby's real name was Tebathia after some Pilgrim ancestor of Mrs. Shreve's, wasn't it? The people around here must have taken a vote two hundred years ago to exclude anyone who hadn't come over on the *Mayflower*. So what? They didn't need Matt and he didn't need them. He kicked a stone across the yard so hard it hurt his toe right through his sneaker.

3

Matt's run-in with the Vosserts and the police was just one more lemon to add to the pile of lemons that had turned out to be Cape Cod. As far as he was concerned, everything about their move had been a bust. It was as if his mother were trying to recapture her youth by dragging Bucky and him back into her past. She had spent every summer of her life here in East Tedham until she and Dad had gotten married and moved to Denver. It was in Denver that Matt had been born. And been happy.

But then nine years ago Dad had been killed in a car accident and everything had changed. Matt was only eight when it happened, but he remembered a whole lot about his father. Most of all he remembered the hunting trips his father had taken him on along with their old spaniel Sarge—the setting out in the predawn darkness, the warm closeness of the long drive, the last star blinking out, the first sighting of wings overhead. With all his memories plus the family photographs and stories, it sometimes seemed as if his father were still around. Most of the time, though, like when he got in trouble for speeding or when the principal of his old high school tried to suspend him for fighting, Matt knew his father wasn't around at all. He just bet his father would have stayed cool instead of getting whipped up like his mother always did.

Shortly after Dad had died, Mom had married Warren Coxe, an airline pilot based in Denver. Bucky was born the following year and everything would have been okay because Matt got along pretty well with Warren, but his mother and Warren couldn't make a go of it. Mom blamed herself, saying she had remarried too quickly and for the wrong reasons and so that was that. As soon as she and Warren were divorced and the house sold, she and Matt and Bucky had moved back here to East Tedham into the vacation house she had inherited from her parents. Now Mom expected Matt and Bucky to be as crazy about Cape Cod as she was.

Who could be crazy about Cape Cod, Matt wondered as he finished the last of his waffles. It was Saturday morning and Mom had made her usual weekend effort of waffles and sausages. Matt usually ate about ten, but since he'd been sick, he couldn't handle more than four. Bucky looked over at Matt triumphantly as he held out his plate for another helping.

Matt had to admit it. Bucky wasn't doing badly. He complained a lot about not seeing his father, but as an airline pilot, Warren had never been around much anyway. Bucky was really well coordinated, and as soon as he had hit his new school, he'd started playing in some peanut hockey league and now he had as many friends as he'd had back in Colorado.

Unfortunately, as soon as Matt had hit *his* new school, the coaches had taken one look at his almost-six-foot height and gone bananas thinking they had a big jock on their hands. What they didn't know but soon found out was that Matt had grown more than five inches in a year and was mentally still five feet six. It made for a lot of tripping over his own feet and bumping into things. Then a month after the move, Matt had gotten mononucleosis which had wiped him out of everything, including getting to know any of the kids. *Especially* out of getting to know any of the kids. Plus, he wasn't allowed to work. Money was tight and he needed a job badly.

"How about me getting an after-school job, Mom?"

"You have a job." Mom poured more batter into the waffle iron and closed the lid. It steamed and hissed and dripped all over the table as usual.

"I'm seventeen. Walking a dog twice a day is for ten-year-olds. I need a real job with real money." Matt had thought it all out. If he got a job now and worked through the summer, he'd not only be able to buy his heart's desire, a Ruger model 77 .270 caliber rifle, but by fall, he'd have enough money to fly back to Colorado for some buck hunting with his old buddies.

"The answer is no, Matt. Why, you can hardly get through the day without falling asleep. When your blood test is normal, then we'll see."

"I could get a job." Bucky was shoveling in the waffles so fast his face was smeared with syrup. Now he looked up and grinned, showing three toothless gaps.

Mom smiled and rubbed Bucky's straight blond hair. "You've got a couple of years to go, honey."

"I could walk Mrs. Shreve's dog if Matt doesn't want to." Bucky poured more syrup on his already soggy waffles.

"Can it, Bucky. You can't even walk to the john alone." Matt pushed his plate away.

"Hey, Mom, did you hear that?" Bucky wailed.

"Cut it out, you two." Mom pushed back the hair that had fallen over her forehead, smearing waffle batter on her eyebrow.

"Is that a promise about the blood test, Mom?" Matt wasn't about to let his mother off the hook.

"It's a promise." Mom held up her hand Indian-fashion. "And when a good job prospect comes into the newspaper, I'll let you know."

Matt's mother worked for the *Cape Cod Tribune* and one of her departments was Want Ads. Although she considered herself to be a journalist and Want Ads beneath her, Matt now realized it was a definite advantage. He'd have a day's jump on everyone else.

He took his down vest from the hook by the back door. "I'd better get over to Mrs. Shreve's. I forgot to lay her wood stove last night and her house will be freezing."

Mom frowned as she started to clear the table. "Do you go to Mrs. Shreve's by way of Uncle Clement's Road?"

Another crazy name. There wasn't a Main Street or Oak Road in the whole town. Matt nodded. "Yeah."

"You know those people at the top of Uncle Clement's Road where you had the trouble last week?" Mom asked. She meant the Vosserts. Matt hadn't planned on telling his mother what had happened, but her mother-sees-all eyes had noticed how angry he'd been when he got home and she had wormed it out of him.

Matt nodded again. "Yeah."

The Vosserts were a strange pair. Not once, in all the times Matt had ridden his bike past, had he seen Mrs. Vossert, although he sometimes saw Mr. Vossert standing at his front window looking out as Matt passed, as if he were keeping an eye on Matt at the same time Matt was keeping an eye on him.

"Well, last night I stopped at their house," Mom continued, "and asked them over for a drink thinking it might made amends for the incident."

"What did they say?" Matt was all interest now.

"*They* didn't say anything. Mr. Vossert came to the door but didn't invite me in. He said he and his wife Sidney, if you can believe that name, had come to East Tedham for a rest and weren't seeing anyone. Then he shut the door in my face." Mom, who was putting away the waffle batter, angrily slammed the fridge door shut. "I wouldn't ask that man over again if he begged me."

Mom's boiling point was low. Like Matt's. They were both tall and brown-eyed too, with the same curly brown hair that kinked up in damp weather, though lately Mom's was streaked with gray. For sure, Bucky didn't look like either of them. He was blond and blue-eyed like Warren.

Matt had been right. Mrs. Shreve's house was cold when he arrived. Matt figured it was so old it probably didn't have much insulation. On the silvered shingles above the front door was lettered the date 1749, which must have been the year it was built. The furniture inside looked as if it had been around since 1749 too. The wide-plank floors were covered with hooked rugs, and every room was crammed with ancient-looking antiques.

As soon as Matt got the fire going, he asked Mrs. Shreve about the Vosserts. It hadn't taken Matt long to realize that Cape Codders knew everything about everybody. Naturally, Mrs. Shreve hadn't called on the Vosserts like Mom had. Cape Codders, apparently, didn't call. Only one person had called on Matt's mother since they had arrived, old Miss Wilson from down the street who had brought not only a jar of beach plum jam with her, but her tiger cat, Bingo, as well. But whether Mrs. Shreve had called or not, Matt counted on her knowing at least something about the Vosserts.

"I've heard tell they're from Arizona and secretive as hermits. Nary a soul has seen Mrs. Vossert since they arrived, and Mr. Vossert isn't visible much either, though when he is, he wears a three-piece suit like he's off to business. Near's I can make out, they don't go to bed 'til midnight. That much I can see from here. But that's the upshot of it." Mrs. Shreve sounded as disappointed by her lack of information as Matt was.

By coincidence, it was only twenty minutes later when Matt was walking Tebby in the marsh that he saw Mr. Vossert out on his deck. Not just Mr. Vossert, but Mrs. Vossert as well. She must have been away all this time, or sick, although she certainly didn't act sick now. Matt remembered the first morning he had met Mrs. Vossert when she had been sitting in her car and Vossert had yelled at her. For sure he wasn't yelling at her today. They had their arms around each other and every once in a while, they embraced in a long kiss.

Now Vossert pointed toward the ocean and Mrs. Vossert smiled and nodded. Then, with his arm still around her, he led her to the south deck and gestured toward the marsh. Again she nodded and acted interested, almost as if she were seeing it for the first time. Hey, the way they were acting, maybe that wasn't Mrs. Vossert at all, but some other woman. It was possible. As far as Matt could remember, Mrs. Vossert had sat really low in her car as if she were short, and this woman was tall, the same height as Vossert.

Unfortunately, at that moment Tebby barked at something down by the sluice bridge and Vossert's head immediately turned in that direction. Now he shaded his eyes and scanned the length of the marsh until he came to Black Rock. And Matt. Even at a distance, Matt could see how he tensed up. He said something to the woman and immediately the two of them hurried back into the house. A moment later, the draperies were pulled shut across the floor-to-ceiling sliding glass doors. And that was that. There was nothing more to see, only the draperies pulled tight and a gray cloud cover moving across the sun, totally blocking out its pale rays.

4

The way Vossert had rushed his wife, or whoever that woman was, inside the house when he realized that Matt was watching them was really strange. What difference did it make whether Matt saw them or not? For the rest of the weekend, every time he walked Tebby, he kept an eye out for the Vosserts, but he didn't catch a glimpse of either one of them, not even half hidden behind the curtain of the front window.

And then it was Monday, raining, with five days of school ahead. By the time lunch period came around, Matt was dragging. He would rather have dropped than admit it, but at that point, what he wanted was sleep, not food. At least he was excused from gym so he could get to the cafeteria ahead of the mob. He and Joe Turnbull just naturally drifted into lunch together. Joe had gotten racked up in a motorcycle accident and couldn't take gym either.

Because neither Matt nor Joe was much of a talker, they were just sitting eating in silence when Julie Chamberlain came up to their table. Matt figured she wanted to talk to Joe. He knew who Julie Chamberlain was because she was in one of his study periods, but he didn't think she knew who he was. Apparently she did. At least she knew his name.

"Hey there, Joe, how're you doing? Hi, Matthew." She put an apple and a carton of yogurt on the table and sat down.

Most of the teachers called him Matthew so that must be where she got the Matthew bit. Matt didn't like it and he wasn't sure he was so crazy about Julie either. She was tall and thin, with long, straight, almost flaxen blond hair and fair skin that reminded him of a Cape Cod icicle. And she was always surrounded by an earnest looking bunch of kids like groupie satellites around a planet.

"Someone told me you're from Colorado, Matthew." She took a piece of gum out of her mouth and stuck it in a paper napkin. Gum completed the picture. He couldn't stand gum-clacking, gum-popping girls.

"Yeah, Denver." Actually he was from Cranford, a little town outside of Denver but it was easier to say Denver. Even Cape Codders had heard of Denver.

"I've never been West in my life. I'd love to see the Rockies and the Grand Canyon and some of our national parks." Julie opened her yogurt and started to eat.

"I went West when I was eleven," Joe interjected. "We hit fifteen states in two weeks and it was a big bore."

Julie laughed. "Joe, you'd be bored on a flight to the moon." Before Joe could retort, Julie turned back to Matt. "We have a little club here at school, Matthew, the John Muir Conservation Club, and we thought it would be real nice if you came to some of our meetings. You don't have to join or anything, but being from the West, we figured you might be interested, plus have a whole lot to offer us. Today we're showing a real good movie. How about it?"

All of a sudden, Matt didn't feel tired any more. In

27

fact, he felt pretty good. This was the first time in the two months since he had moved to Cape Cod that anyone had asked him to do anything except donate blood which was the one thing he couldn't do. As far as he was concerned, Cape Cod was a perfect name. Everyone was about as friendly as a catch of cold codfish. Now Julie Chamberlain, who if not big around school, was at least bigger than he was, had not only spoken to him but asked him to come to a meeting.

"Sure, why not? As a matter of fact, I've traveled around the West quite a lot and taken some pretty good pictures," Matt said, trying to sound both interesting and modest at the same time. Besides, it was true. He did have some good pictures. He'd gotten an Olympus XA 2 for his fifteenth birthday and, to his surprise and everyone else's, he had turned out to have a real knack for photography.

Julie stood up. "Great. See you in Room 325 after eighth period."

As soon as Julie was gone, Joe clapped Matt on the back. "Hey, I'm impressed. Julie Chamberlain doesn't usually run around throwing herself at guys."

"She wasn't exactly throwing herself at me." Maybe she wasn't, but Matt felt as flattered as if she had been.

There were about fifteen kids in the meeting room when Matt arrived. Room 325 was the biology lab. Plants grew on the windowsills, pickled animals and reptiles curled up in cloudy jars and various forms of squealing rodents scratched in metal cages. Outside sheets of rain swept across an empty field and slapped against the windows. Two buckets had been placed under leaks in the ceiling and water plip-plopped into them in a steady rhythm. Matt had long ago decided that weather was never simple around here. If there was rain, it was a torrent. If a wind blew, it was a gale.

"Hi, Matthew." A smiling Julie led Matt over to a group of kids sitting around on desk tops. She produced a box of doughnuts from somewhere and passed them around as she introduced Matt.

"This is Matthew Runyon who's moved here from Colorado. This is Phoebe and Sarah and Tim and Jake and Phil and . . ." It was hopeless. Matt just nodded at everyone, not even trying to get their names straight.

"Hey, Julie, what's wrong with this projector?" someone called from across the room. "I don't think Mr. Anton-baby set it up right."

Julie seemed to be in charge. "Nothing's wrong with it, Tozzi. I just checked it out." She headed for Tozzi and the projector, leaving Matt with Tim and Jake and whoever the rest of them were.

"So you're from Colorado?" one of the girls asked, taking a bite of doughnut that left her mouth ringed with white.

"Yeah, Denver."

"Did you belong to the John Muir Conservation Club out there?"

"No, I don't even think there was one."

"You're kidding. The way Denver needs a conservation program? I heard it's one of the fastest growing cities in the West with the worst pollution."

"Well, you heard wrong. Their pollution isn't half as bad as the fog, smog, rain and humidity around here," Matt countered. "And Denver doesn't need help from anyone. That just means hotshots coming in and saying no more mining, no more lumbering, no more hunting."

There was a moment of stunned silence with the only sound in the room the alternating pings of water hitting the buckets. One of the girls broke the silence. "Hunting. You hunt?"

"I don't around here because Massachusetts has such stupid gun laws, but as soon as I'm eighteen and can get my permit I will. I don't know anyone back home who doesn't go for their buck every fall. They count on a buck for winter meat. Ducks, geese, pheasant, quail too. And fish. I suppose you object to fishing, or are those pleasure boats I see going out every morning?"

"Hey, Runyon, you don't have to go off the deep end." That was Tim.

"I guess I get fed up with Easterners always telling Westerners what to do. We're not idiots, believe it or not."

"Ayuh, if you're not an idiot, then how come you walk that dog of yours in Nimicut Salt Marsh every day?" Matt remembered that one's name was Jake. Jake angrily stuffed the last half of a doughnut in his mouth, then reached for another. By now most of the other kids were looking pretty hostile too.

"What are you talking about?"

"Don't you know what you're doing to the ecology by letting that dog loose in the marsh?" Jake jutted out his jaw belligerently.

"No, I don't. Not only that, but I don't care."

Jake stood up. He was tall, taller even than Matt, and heavier. "You and your dog are demolishing that marsh. You might as well come in and bulldoze it."

"If I had a bulldozer that's just what I'd do."

Now Matt and Jake were facing each other off like some cornball duel in a late-night movie, with everyone else circled around them. Matt, with half a doughnut still in his hand, was at a distinct disadvantage. He put it down and shoved his fists in his pockets.

"Hey, hey, hey." It was Julie picking up the doughnut box and holding it between them like a wedge. "I don't believe this scene. What's with you guys anyway?"

"This jerk won't listen to . . ."

"It's nobody's business where I walk . . ."

They had both answered at once. Matt's scalp prickled and his ears flushed the way they did when he was losing control. Who were these creeps to tell him what he could or couldn't do?

"Come on and sit down, Matthew. And you, Jake, cool it. Tozzi's about to start the movie." Julie pulled at Matt's arm so that he didn't have any choice but to follow her to the first row of desks. It was just as well. In another minute, he'd have punched Jake and in the kind of shape he was in, Jake would have pulverized him. He picked up the rest of his doughnut and ate it, though the thick smell of formaldehyde in the stuffy room was beginning to make him sick.

Someone lowered the shades, blotting out the rain weeping down the windows, and the movie began. It was jerky and the sound track wasn't very good, and though Matt was a little slow on the uptake, he got the message soon enough. The title of the film was *Can We Save Our Salt Marshes?* with an appropriate musical score and forebodings of doom from the baritone narrator about the beauty of salt marshes and how they are the nurseries of the sea and a vital zone of mediation between sea and land and how developers are destroying them and   .   .   .

And Matt had had enough. He jumped up and pushed himself away from his desk so furiously the empty doughnut box toppled to the floor, scattering crumbs and powdered sugar. The room was dark and he bumped into a couple of desks as he stumbled his way toward the door. He yanked it open, blinked a moment at the bright light, then headed down the hall.

"Matthew, hey, Matthew, wait for me."

It was Julie running after him, her clogs clacking on the polished floor and echoing in the empty halls. Matt didn't even turn around.

"Matthew, you can't go like that." Julie grabbed Matt's arm just as he reached the exit door.

Stopping Matt was her mistake. He hadn't planned on

saying anything. He was too angry to handle words and he knew it. But now she'd asked for it. He jerked his arm away.

"First of all, no one calls me Matthew, not ever and that includes you. Second, you Cape Cod codfish can't push me around just because you think I'm a jerkwater hick from the West." Matt was almost shouting. "Why didn't you just come out and ask me not to walk my dog in the marsh instead of all that a.k.-ing about me coming to a meeting because I have so much to offer. As far as I'm concerned, you can bag your movie and bag your precious marsh too. I'll do what I want."

"Please come back, Matt. For me."

No, he'd let himself be taken in once and that was enough. For an answer, he pushed the door open and rushed out into the parking lot. It was still pouring. The rain seemed to come from every direction as it whipped across the empty fields. There were no trees to soften its fury, only low shrubbery and an occasional pitch pine. Bleak. Desolate. Like everything else around here.

Even worse, all the school buses had left. That meant he'd have to wait for the late bus. All of a sudden Matt was not only wet, but tired too. Not just tired. Dead tired. He couldn't stand the thought of waiting around for another hour and a half. He'd hitchhike home, that's what he'd do. Maybe he'd get mugged the way his mother was always predicting he would. After all, he'd already gotten one mugging today, he might as well try for two.

5

"*H*i, Matt."

Matt spun around. Julie Chamberlain had come up the path behind him so silently he hadn't even heard her. She wore running shoes and an old pair of blue jeans, with her long blond hair pulled back in a single thick braid. Her hair was cobwebbed with the same fine halo of moisture as Tebby's black coat. Matt still wasn't sure whether it was raining, misting or if there was just so much humidity in the air it clung to everything. A Jack-in-the-mist fog, Mrs. Shreve had called it.

"What a nice black Lab. What's her name?" Julie stroked Tebby's head.

"Tebby."

Julie hunkered down and rubbed Tebby's neck and broad chest, causing Tebby's tail to go like a metronome. "Hey, look at her paws. Her toes are joined."

"All Labs have webbed paws. They use them for swimming, like ducks." Matt's tone was curt.

Julie must have known his routine and shown up just to meet him. Matt had cooled off some since the Muir

Club meeting, but not a hundred percent. He yanked on Tebby's leash and kept going toward the marsh. Julie followed.The path was so narrow the prickly briar bushes plucked at their legs, forcing Julie to walk behind him single file.

"I'm really sorry about what happened, Matt." Julie raised her voice so he'd be sure to hear. "We didn't try to mislead you, honest. We just wanted you to understand what a fragile environment a salt marsh is and how easily its ecology can be thrown off balance."

"Okay, fine. Now I know. Let's forget the whole thing."

"You don't sound as if you think it's fine."

Matt shrugged but didn't respond. They had reached Black Rock. Matt had labeled it Bad Day at Black Rock the afternoon Dr. Grogan told him he had mono. Now it was later in the day than usual and Tebby was frantic to run. It somehow gave Matt great satisfaction to release the catch on her leash and let her take off into the marsh. The fingers of the incoming tide were just beginning to stretch their way up the dry creek beds like something alive, twisting and probing. Tebby hit the shallow water at full speed.

Neither Matt nor Julie said anything as they watched her streak for the east end of the marsh down by the sluice dam where the water, flowing in from the ocean by way of several meandering channels, cascaded into the marsh in one giant flume. Something down by the sluice dam must have attracted her. Every day this week she had headed in that direction, prowling and sniffing around.

Julie had a pair of small binoculars around her neck. Now she dried off the lenses with her sweatshirt, exposing a pale expanse of skin before she raised the binoculars in Tebby's direction. "I can't see what Tebby is after, but I know there's a family of foxes living somewhere in the marsh. I hope she's not after them."

That's probably just what she was after. Every time

Matt had seen the fox, he was in the vicinity of the sluice dam. Not that Matt was about to tell Julie.

Tebby must have given up her quest because she now ran full tilt toward the far side of the marsh, barking at some new unseen treasure.

"Have you thought about walking Tebby on the beach? She'd love the ocean," Julie asked casually.

Apparently Julie hadn't given up on trying to get Tebby out of the marsh. She had probably made Matt and Tebby her special Muir Club project. One thing for sure, she wasn't going to have any luck on the beach business. Matt had taken Tebby there once and he'd hated the whole experience.

The ocean had been one vast, gray, white-capped pounding fury and the sea wind was so raw and cold it had penetrated right through his down vest, sweater, shirt and T-shirt in a way that even below-zero temperatures never did in Colorado. The beach had been littered with mounds of seaweed and driftwood and horseshoe crab shells and other debris washed up by the tide, including the remains of a small dead seal. Huge gulls had wheeled and dipped overhead, screaming at Matt and Tebby as if to drive them away. It was true that Tebby had loved the ocean, cold as it was, but the whole scene was so desolate and depressing that Matt had never gone back.

Even here in the marsh he could see the dancing, cold white caps and hear the endless thunder of the surf. "I don't like the beach. Or the ocean either," he said, wiping the moisture from his face with the back of his sleeve.

It was as if he had announced he burned the American flag for a hobby. Julie looked aghast. "Why, I can't get through a day without touching base with the sea. I run on the beach twice a day no matter what the weather. The sea is the most powerful force in the world . . . it's part of my life . . . in my blood . . . I . . . I couldn't live without it." She was almost stuttering.

35

"I miss the mountains."

Matt hadn't planned on saying that. The words had just come out. But as soon as he said them, he knew he did miss the mountains. He missed their grandeur, their permanence and stability, the way they were always the same and yet always different, depending on the mood of the weather and the time of day or season of the year. He missed the smell of the big pines and the clean forests underfoot that were layered with needles. To Matt's horror, his eyes brimmed with tears. He knew it was the mono that had left him so weak and shaky, but he was mortified.

If Julie noticed, she pretended not to. She put the binoculars up to her eyes and gazed out over the marsh, giving him time to pull himself together.

"Oh, Matt, look at that flock of plovers. They're our earliest migrators north, a real sign of spring." She handed Matt the binoculars and pointed to the far side of the marsh.

It took Matt a moment to adjust the lens and find the birds. Suddenly they jumped into circled focus, a whole flock of small shorebirds, dark brown above and white below, poking in the mud of the tidal creeks with sharp little beaks. They certainly weren't anything special that Matt could see. He was about to lower his binoculars when Julie grabbed his arm.

"There's the fox." She was whispering. "Over there, by the sluice bridge. Quick, call Tebby back."

Sure enough, the fox was down near the bridge where Matt had seen him before. Now, through binoculars, Matt could clearly see the snow-white fur on the fox's throat and chest, and black fur like stockings on his long legs. His bushy tail flowed gracefully behind him. Tebby had seen him too. She was running full speed toward the sluice bridge, her ears pricked up in anticipation.

Julie jumped up and down. "Call Tebby! Quick!"

Matt whistled. "Here, Tebby. Come, girl." He made the effort more to keep Julie from getting hysterical than from any hope that Tebby would obey.

Obviously Tebby had no intention of obeying. She barked once and took off after the fox. The fox paused, his whole body alert and his big ears pointed straight up. Then he darted across one of the creeks with Tebby right behind him. In a moment, both of them had disappeared behind a low hummock of brown grass. There was a quick flash of black that was Tebby's tail, but there was no sign of the fox at all. Now Tebby's head poked up from behind the hummock. She seemed confused as she cocked her head first in one direction, then another. When she came out from behind the hummock, she raced across the creek into the grass, paused, then ran back across the creek again. She seemed almost frantic.

Julie's laughter was partly in humor but mostly in relief. "Do you see what that fox is doing? The female must have a litter of pups in the den and the male is luring Tebby away by using himself as bait. By circling back, he's almost got Tebby crazy."

Matt didn't want to have anything in common with Julie, but when Tebby looked over at them with a how-could-this-happen-to-such-a-clever-dog-as-me look, Matt couldn't help laughing himself.

His laughter was like a signal Julie had been waiting for. "I'd better get going or I'll be late for dinner. Keep the binoculars and bring them to school tomorrow."

Matt ripped the binoculars from around his neck and held them out. "No, here, you take them."

But Julie had already started jogging down the path that led toward the beach. Matt watched her cross the rickety little bridge over the sluice dam where the tide was pouring in, and then she was out of sight behind the dunes.

Matt didn't want to get involved with Julie in any

way. He hadn't even planned on talking to her. Now she'd hoodwinked him a second time with a pair of binoculars that had to be returned. Matt was so furious at himself for letting Julie manipulate him he wasn't sure if he'd ever give them back. He dropped them around his neck angrily, then changed his mind. Since he was stuck with the binoculars, he might as well use them. He raised them to his eyes and swung them toward Bluff Cottage.

There was no sign of the Vosserts, and as usual the draperies were all pulled shut. All but one. At the far end of the house one was opened just a crack. Now the red ball of the setting sun in the west flashed off something bright inside. Matt focused on the light. He sucked in his breath with a shock of surprise. Vossert was standing inside his house looking out the window through a pair of binoculars that had caught the last of the sun's rays. And his binoculars were trained right on Matt. Wow, Vossert must have been watching Julie and him this whole time. Matt quickly lowered his binoculars at the same time the Bluff Cottage drapery dropped back in place and Vossert disappeared from view.

6

When Matt finally returned Julie's binoculars, she tried to get a conversation going with him, but he wasn't interested. Although he knew perfectly well that all she wanted was to get Tebby and him out of her precious marsh, he had to give her credit for perseverance. Every time they ran into each other in school, she seemed really glad to see him. Suprisingly enough, some of the Muir Club kids acted okay too. Matt figured they were either embarrassed by the way they'd conned him, or, and more likely, they wanted to win him over the way Julie did so he'd stay away from the marsh.

Despite their attempts at brainwashing, or perhaps because of them, Matt continued to walk Tebby in Nimicut Salt Marsh. It was a free country, wasn't it? By now Tebby considered it her home turf and as far as Matt was concerned, it was the perfect place to keep an eye on Bluff Cottage. Ever since the day Vossert had been watching him from behind his draperies, Matt had taken his mother's binoculars to the marsh with him. They weren't as powerful as Julie's but they suited his purpose fine. He set himself up behind Black Rock at the south edge of the marsh. It made a perfect blind with a clear view of Bluff Cottage to the north.

But after that one weird dual-binocular exchange, Matt never caught Vossert watching him again. Still, Matt continued his surveillance. Although the draperies stayed closed so he couldn't see into the house, occasionally the Vosserts appeared on their deck or in their backyard. Every once in a while, Vossert drove out in his Cadillac, but always alone and never for long. To be honest, Matt had to admit that none of the Vosserts' behavior was particularly unusual except for the fact that whenever they were together, they couldn't keep their hands off each other. After watching them kiss and embrace one afternoon for what seemed like an eternity, Matt finally decided that the woman wasn't Mrs. Vossert. It was one thing to be all over your wife the day she returned from being away or maybe recovered from being sick, but Matt knew enough about marriage to realize it was definitely another thing for a husband and wife to go on like that day after day. No, it was clear to him that Mrs. Vossert was out of the picture and this woman, whoever she was, was in.

When there wasn't anything to watch at Bluff Cottage, which was most of the time, Matt watched the comings and goings in the marsh. In particular he kept an eye out for the fox. But the fox was elusive and clever and Matt only glimpsed him once or twice.

If Matt didn't see much of the fox, he saw plenty of the resident marsh hawk. The hawks in Colorado were larger and more impressive, but for some reason, this one caught Matt's fancy. It cruised low over the salt marsh by the hour, hunting rodents and small birds and whatever it could catch. Sometimes it dove seven or eight times before coming up with anything in its powerful talons. It was patient and tenacious, that old hawk, and Matt came to admire it.

And then there was the day the Canada geese stopped over. What a sight that was. When Matt and Tebby arrived at the marsh, there must have been hundreds of them, all squawking and gabbling, big, fat Canadian honkers on their way north. More wavering V-lines flew high overhead, their trumpeting call winging back on the north wind like a pack of baying hounds. At the sight of the big birds, Matt realized that Nimicut Salt Marsh must be on the Atlantic Flyway. He'd gone hunting with his father and their spaniel Sarge for Canadian honkers more times than he could remember. Good times, when the fall air was crisp and cold with a bite to it and he and his dad would start out before dawn fortified with thermoses of hot chocolate, returning exhausted hours later with geese for Mom's food locker. What he wouldn't give for a shotgun right now. POW! POW!

But above all and more important than anything else, as spring gradually greened up the dead brown of the winter marsh and melted the salt crusts of ice, Matt began to feel better. It wasn't as if he woke up one morning ready to lick the world, but at the end of the day he didn't feel totally done in the way he used to, and he wasn't falling asleep every night doing his homework either. All of a sudden, buying a Ruger 77 rifle and hunting in Colorado didn't seem like such an unattainable goal, and for the first time since he'd gotten sick, he didn't mind getting his blood test. But the days between having the test and hearing the results seemed like an eternity, especially Friday, when Dr. Grogan was due to call with his report.

To his surprise when he got home on Friday afternoon, Matt found his mother sitting at the kitchen table eating a big dish of ice cream. It was a bad sign. Not only was she home early, but she only ate ice cream when she was upset. And she must have left work in a hurry. She still had typewriter ribbon ink on her fingers and a smudge on her cheek.

41

He didn't even respond to her hello. "Has Dr. Grogan called yet?"

"No, was he supposed to?" She kept on eating.

How could she forget? Matt dropped his books and down vest on the kitchen counter next to the stack of still-dirty breakfast dishes, opened the freezer and pulled out the ice cream carton. Yesterday it had been three quarters full and now it was nearly empty.

"What's up, Mom?" Matt dished himself some and sat down to eat it.

His mother didn't answer for a moment, and for the first time Matt realized by the way she was attacking her ice cream that she was angry as well as upset. "Warren is going to start custody proceedings for Bucky." She put down her spoon and looked at Matt with frightened eyes as if she couldn't believe what she had just said.

Matt couldn't believe it either. Custody proceedings! Did that mean Bucky might have to live with Warren? Matt and Bucky fought a lot. Since moving here they'd had to share a bedroom and Bucky's junk all over the room and his constant chatter were a big nuisance. But the thought of Bucky leaving stunned Matt like a karate chop. All of a sudden his chocolate chip mint ice cream tasted like soggy moss sprinkled with pebbles, and he pushed it away.

"Bucky would never want to live with Warren, would he?" Matt's eyes met his mother's as he realized how much *he* wanted to move back to Colorado. Even though Bucky seemed to have made a terrific adjustment to East Tedham, maybe he felt the same way.

Matt's mother ignored the question as if she couldn't even contemplate the possibility. "Warren married Diane Hall last week, that little redhead who worked in the photography shop, remember? She's at least fifteen years younger than Warren. Fifteen years." Mom practically choked on the words. "Warren now claims that he and his little wife can provide a more stable home for Bucky than I can. Stable home. That's a laugh." Mom ate the last of her ice cream, then reached for the carton and scooped out the sodden remains.

"What are you going to do?"

"Nothing for now. I called a lawyer in Provincetown and he advised me to sit tight until the case is heard formally. But to do nothing is almost more than I can stand, especially since I know perfectly well that Diane doesn't want any part of being saddled with Bucky." Mom ran her fingers through her short curly hair.

The phone rang and she jumped up. "Maybe that's my lawyer. He said he'd get back to me."

"Oh yes, Dr. Grogan . . . I see . . . all right . . . yes, thanks for calling."

There it was. The results of the blood test. Matt's eyes searched Mom's face, silently pleading.

She shook her head gently as she hung up. "I'm sorry, Matt. That was Dr. Grogan and though your blood test was better, it still isn't normal. For the time being everything is status quo."

"I don't believe it!" Matt's fist came down so hard on the table, his ice cream bowl jumped. "I feel fine. There's nothing wrong with me that I can't handle a job."

Mom shook her head again. "No, Matt. I'm sorry. You know our bargain."

Matt pushed his chair back, grabbed his down vest from the counter, the car keys off the hook on the back door and slammed out of the house. He had to get out before he exploded. Lousy blood test. Lousy mono. Lousy custody proceedings. Most of all, lousy Cape Cod. None of this would have happened if they'd stayed in Colorado. None of it.

7

Matt drove aimlessly around East Tedham's winding streets. Not that there was anything to see. Every street looked like every other. Empty fields punctuated by an occasional stunted tree were interspersed with weathered gray-shingled cottages folded neatly in behind low shrubbery, shuttered up now like toy jack-in-the-boxes waiting to be sprung open. Matt knew when he got home his mother would let him have it for taking the car without permission, but he was so angry and frustrated, he just had to have wheels under him and be moving, even if it was only in the beat-up old Plymouth. He'd already been driving over half an hour when he noticed that he was near Mrs. Shreve's house. Well, since he was due to walk Tebby anyway, he might as well stop and get it over with.

When Mrs. Shreve opened the door, Tebby leapt all over Matt in anticipation of her walk. "You're early, Matt." Mrs. Shreve stepped back to let him in. "I just made a pot of tea after cooking my weekly crock of baked beans. Join me in a cup."

Mrs. Shreve swung her walker toward the molassesey-smelling kitchen with Matt following. He still didn't trust himself to speak. With her usual tact, Mrs. Shreve didn't comment. She just took down two cups, poured tea from a silver teapot, placed everything on a silver tray and asked him to carry it into the parlor. The tray was heavy. And obviously valuable. The way things were going today, he'd probably trip over his own feet and drop everything. But he managed, and the two of them sat down with their tea. The wood stove was throwing so much heat into the little room, Matt peeled off his sweater as Mrs. Shreve took a sip of tea, closed her eyes and leaned her head back.

"It's probably absurd to bake beans every week when getting about is such a chore, but, pshaw, if I give up my Saturday beans, I've given up everything," she said.

"I don't like baked beans." Actually Matt liked them okay, but right now he wasn't in a mood to be positive about anything.

Mrs. Shreve opened her eyes and smiled at him. "You haven't eaten my beans. Come around tomorrow and I'll give you some. It's a family recipe that goes back over a hundred years, and a family tradition. Hot baked beans and brown bread on Saturday night, with cold baked beans for Sunday lunch after church. Father even baked beans when he was in the Yukon."

"You mean during the Gold Rush?" Despite himself, as an old Jack London fan, Matt was impressed.

Mrs. Shreve rearranged a few hairpins, but her hair was so fine and thin it wisped around her face like a halo. "Ayuh, Father took off for the Yukon when he was twenty. He lost four toes from frostbite and panned just enough gold to get him back here to East Tedham. He married Mother soon after, but he always had the wanderlust. Before you could say Obadiah Brown, Father was off to some exotic place leaving Mother to run the family coal business and raise us children alone. I can't say I ever knew Father very well."

Surprisingly, the tea tasted hot and good and at last

Matt's heart had stopped its crazy beating. Tebby had settled down by the stove, her satiny head resting on her paws and her hazel eyes half closed.

"I didn't know my father very well either. He was . . . was killed in an accident." Even now it was hard for Matt to talk about it.

"I know, Matt, I'm sorry." Mrs. Shreve sipped her tea.

Matt sipped his tea too, not sure how far he wanted to go. "Maybe if my father was around now, everything wouldn't be in such a mess. We used to go hunting together. It's what I liked to do best with my dad," Matt began.

Mrs. Shreve didn't say anything. She just poured herself more tea and held out the pot for Matt to come get more too.

As Matt stood up, his thoughts were back in Colorado with his father and he didn't notice the footstool in front of him. He tripped and almost fell, catching his teacup just in time. As soon as he'd gotten a fresh cup and returned to his chair, he knew he had to get everything out or burst. "My stepfather is trying to get custody of my stepbrother Bucky and Mom's off the wall about it. And I've had mononucleosis practically since we moved here and I don't think I'll ever be over it and I can't get a full-time job and I don't know any kids and don't care about knowing any kids and all I want is to go back to Colorado where I belong." There it was, all unloaded and dumped between them like a heap of rubbish.

Mrs. Shreve didn't comment for a moment. Then she leaned forward and her pale blue eyes bored into Matt's brown ones. "You appear very angry about it all, Matt." Her one eyebrow went up as if she were asking a question.

"Why shouldn't I be? Everything's gone wrong and

it's all because of our stupid move back here. I had plenty of friends in Colorado."

"I'm sorry, Matt. I wish I could help, but as you can see, I'm a pretty helpless ol' gal." Indicating the knee-to-foot cast under the afghan robe, Mrs. Shreve smiled ruefully. "I don't even know what it's like to move someplace else. This house was our family homestead even before I was born. All I've knowledge about is baked beans and cranberry glass and swimming. I know you don't care about baked beans and cranberry glass, Matt, but what about swimming? Have you ever swum in the ocean?"

"No, and I don't ever want to."

"That's a pity. Here on Cape Cod you're never more'n six miles away from the ocean anywhere you might be. I love the ocean and always have. At the time everyone thought Father was daft, but he taught all us children to swim. 'Course, in those days no one around here knew how to swim but oh, how we loved it. I still swim every day in the summer and I'm hoping swimming will help this devilish leg of mine, come warm weather."

Mrs. Shreve finished her tea, put down her cup and picked up a piece of needlepoint. It was a picture of some kind of boat on a bright blue sea. "Anyway," she continued, "over a long lifetime I've learned a lot about surviving in the water. When I swim against the waves, I just get all knocked about. If I attack one wave and conquer it, there's always another right behind it and fighting wave after wave is like trying to run up a down escalator." Mrs. Shreve cut the blue yarn and threaded her needle with white.

The funny thing was that Matt knew just what she was talking about. He'd once tried to run up a down escalator and it had not only been exhausting, but it had taken forever. He nodded, his eyes on a dour and forbidding gentleman whose portrait hung behind Mrs. Shreve's chair.

47

"So I try to relax and ride with the waves and let the ocean do the work, buoying me up and carrying me along. And if I ever get caught in a riptide or strong current, I swim parallel to the shore 'til I can work in through the surf at an angle. Fear and panic can defeat you too."

Mrs. Shreve looked over at Matt and smiled, the deep crow's feet around her eyes forking out symmetrically. "You might want to try ocean swimming come summer, Matt. I think you'd like it."

Matt shifted his eyes from the portrait to Mrs. Shreve. "Maybe," he hedged.

"Good. Now how about taking Tebby out before she scratches my front door down? She knows it's time for her walk."

Matt checked his watch. Sure enough, it was exactly the time he usually took Tebby for her walk. He quickly got up, took down her leash from the hook, and waved a good-bye to Mrs. Shreve. As he and Tebby headed for the marsh, he realized that Mrs. Shreve hadn't given him any concrete advice, nor was anything more settled than before, but for some reason, he felt a whole lot better.

For once, the Vosserts were the farthest thing from Matt's mind as he released Tebby for her run. So when he saw Vossert directly across the marsh just down a bit from Bluff Cottage, it caught him up short. Even though it was cold out, cold enough for Matt to see his breath, Vossert was wearing only a business suit. But stranger than that, he was smoothing out a place between two pitch pines with a shovel as if he had just been digging. As Matt watched, Vossert tamped the earth down over and over with his shovel, then, leaning down, he lifted a big pick off the ground. His breath puffed in little quick clouds of exertion as he started up the hill toward his house with the pick and shovel over his shoulder.

Fascinated, Matt continued to watch Vossert's progress as he vanished behind a tangle of briars and winter-

curled blackberry bushes. Moments later, Vossert reappeared on his back porch. Propping the pick and shovel
against the side of the house, he opened the back door, but
just before going in, he hesitated. He was a good distance
away so Matt couldn't be sure, but he thought Vossert
glanced over across the marsh in his direction before he
disappeared inside his house.

8

Matt didn't want to miss his after-school bus on Tuesday. He had to get home, pick up Bucky and the car, then drive to Dr. Grogan's for Bucky's allergy shot and his blood test. He wasn't all that hopeful that this test would come out any better than the others, but still, he didn't want to be late. So when Julie Chamberlain stopped him in the hall after eighth period, he wasn't much interested in idle chatter.

"You've been avoiding me like I'm contagious." Julie was clacking away at gum and Matt wondered how she got away with it. Chewing gum drove teachers crazy.

"I've been busy," Matt said. The lie of the century.

Julie fell into step with him. It was a strange feeling to walk beside a girl almost as tall as he was, although Matt had to admit that it made him feel a whole lot less awkward. And she was close enough so that he could smell her freshly shampooed hair. To cover his embarrassment, he ran a pencil along the metal lockers that lined the hall, thwacking each one in turn as he waited for Julie to start the conversation.

Apparently she hadn't stopped him for idle chatter.

She seemed embarrassed too and didn't look at him as she plunged ahead. "Paul Halley's mother works for Dr. Grogan and . . . and . . . Paul says you're always going in for blood tests, that you're having one today. Some of the guys say . . ."—she cleared her throat—". . . some of the guys think you have leukemia . . ." Her voice trailed off.

Leukemia. Matt was having enough trouble with mononucleosis. He stopped so abruptly, two girls walking behind them bumped into him. "Terrific, and who started that charming rumor?"

"You mean you don't have it?" Julie sounded relieved.

"I've got mono, plain, old, simple mono. So 'the guys' know what they can do with their leukemia."

Julie scowled. "Hey, take it easy. No one was trying to spread rumors. You don't take gym or go out for a sport and you've been absent a whole lot and we were worried about you. Take it or leave it as far as I'm concerned."

"I'll leave it, thanks."

Before Julie could come up with a retort, a girl Matt didn't know burst in between them. "Hey, Julie, are you going to Will Nolan's party on Friday night?"

"No, I'm going to Wendy's."

Julie turned to speak to Matt but he had already slipped away. He had almost been ready to make some kind of amends for blowing like that about the leukemia, but he obviously wasn't included in this new conversation. Let them discuss their parties all day as far as he was concerned. But two parties on a Friday night? He had never even been invited to one. Not that he would have gone. He could just imagine what their parties were like—everyone sitting around discussing nuclear disarmament. Well, bag their parties. He had to hurry.

The hurrying was a waste of time. When he and Bucky arrived at Dr. Grogan's office, the waiting room was jammed. Bucky, who was used to doctors' waiting rooms, settled down on the sofa with a comic book. Bucky was allergic to just about everything that walked, flew, bit or swam, and had been getting shots for years. Matt pulled out the new issue of *Guns* magazine that he'd brought with him and started to read too.

They had already been waiting forty-five minutes when Matt heard the nurse in the outer office reassure a new arrival. "Dr. Grogan is running a little late, Mrs. Vossert, but it shouldn't take too long."

At the sound of the name, Matt's head shot up. Sure enough, Vossert was standing in the doorway with the woman. Only it seemed the woman was Mrs. Vossert after all. Certainly that was what the nurse had called her. Matt had been so positive she wasn't the Mrs. Vossert he had first met, he was really surprised.

It was strange, too, to see the Vosserts close up so soon after that weird act of Vossert's with the pick and shovel the other afternoon. To make it even stranger, Mrs. Vossert walked over and sat down next to Bucky on the sofa. Although she glanced first at Bucky and then at Matt, there wasn't a flicker of recognition. Not that there was any reason she should recognize Matt. She had seen him for only about thirty seconds that day she had arrived when she was sitting in her car. If Matt hadn't been watching the Vosserts through binoculars all this time, he wouldn't have recognized her either. Certainly he wouldn't have recognized her from that first day when she'd been wearing big smoked glasses and a scarf over her head.

For sure, Vossert recognized Matt. As soon as Vossert saw him, a flush started at his jawline and suffused his whole face. Immediately, he looked away and took a chair across the room.

"I'm getting an allergy shot," Bucky announced to Mrs. Vossert, a loud voice in the overheated waiting-room silence.

52

Mrs. Vossert didn't respond in any way. She just sat there.

"I'm allergic to bee stings, penicillin, dust, orange juice, chocolate, whole milk, strawberries and all seafood," Bucky rattled off his list. "Are you allergic too? Is that why your arms are all over hives?"

Matt cringed. If he had been sitting closer, he would have kicked Bucky. As it was, he and everyone else in the room looked at Mrs. Vossert's arms and the ugly red welts that covered them.

"It's not hives," Mrs. Vossert snapped. "It's poison ivy."

"Does it itch?" By now Bucky was practically in her lap.

"Bucky, mind your own business," Matt hissed.

Bucky took one look at Matt's disapproving frown and went back to his comic book. But Matt found himself continuing to stare at Mrs. Vossert. There was something about her that drew his attention, but he had no idea what it was. Of course she wasn't wearing all that jewelry she'd had on when he first met her, but with a case of poison ivy like that, why would she?

Although Matt tried his best to concentrate on *Guns*, something about Mrs. Vossert kept drawing him back like a magnet. It was really annoying not to be able to figure out what it was. As he distractedly rubbed his thumbnail between his front teeth he happened to look up. And he met Vossert's steely dark eyes. Vossert was watching Matt watch his wife and he seemed angry about it. More than angry. In that split second of connection, Matt saw alarm in Vossert's eyes too.

Vossert blinked first, looked away, then stood up and strode out to the nurse's station. "How much longer do we have to wait?"

"It'll be another forty-five minutes, I'm afraid, Mr. Vossert."

Vossert immediately reappeared in the doorway. "Sidney." His voice was low but commanding and again everyone in the waiting room followed his progress across the room. "We're leaving. If a man can't keep his appointments, then I refuse to waste my time."

Mrs. Vossert seemed distressed. "But I need relief."

"We're leaving, Sidney." And don't argue, his tone implied.

With that, they were gone. For a while Matt tried to read. But after he'd gone over the same page three times, he gave up. Vossert's insistence that they leave had nothing to do with Dr. Grogan running late, Matt was sure of it. No, it had to do with the way he had been staring at Mrs. Vossert. Vossert hadn't liked that one bit. More than that, it had panicked him into leaving.

"Are you deaf, Matt?" Bucky was poking him. "The nurse is calling your name."

She certainly was. Matt got up and followed her. He had almost forgotten why he was here.

9

Matt woke up the next day before the alarm went off, which almost never happened. Part of the reason was that the spring mornings were growing lighter, but mostly it was because of what had happened in Dr. Grogan's waiting room the day before. Matt *knew* something was wrong with Mrs. Vossert. It was sitting right at the top of his head, but the harder he tried to pin it down, the more elusive it became. Their next-door neighbor back in Cranford used to say that for every year he got older, his memory slipped back two notches. Right now, Matt felt himself going senile the same way. For sure he'd take his binoculars with him to the marsh this morning.

Matt pedaled like mad on his way to Mrs. Shreve's just to keep warm. Because the sun was out bright, he had been deceived into wearing only a sweater. But a stiff east wind gusted and the temperature was low enough for Matt to see his breath. What a climate. Although Colorado got lots of weather too, the mountains acted as a kind of buffer so that every shift of the wind and change in the barometer wasn't as traumatic as it was here by the ocean. Everything about this seashore climate was more variable, more extreme, as if the ocean arbitrarily manufactured its own weather, reducing everything to smaller than life, flattening out the dunes, stunting the trees, paring down the people into a leathery, spare gruffness.

Cold weather or no cold weather, as soon as Matt reached Black Rock and released Tebby, she took off gleefully into the water just as if the creek banks weren't filmed with ice. Matt rubbed his numb hands together and blew into them before pulling out his binoculars and training them on Bluff Cottage. Hey, that was a surprise. In all the weeks he had been keeping an eye on the Vosserts, he had never seen the draperies open on their sliding glass doors. Now they were pulled back all the way so he could see right into their living room.

In delicious anticipation, like saving the biggest Christmas present until last, Matt slowly and deliberately readjusted his binoculars to get the best possible focus. As he looked toward Bluff Cottage, the living room jumped into a perfect circled view, like a stage setting all lit up when the curtain is raised. For a small house, the living room was big, with a high ceiling and not much furniture. And right in the middle of the set was Mrs. Vossert, wearing a yellow housecoat and seated in a low chair drinking from a coffee cup. She seemed to be watching TV. At least Matt could see the blue-and-white flicker of a TV set across the room.

As he slowly scanned the rest of the room, he spotted Vossert coming into the living room through a door to the right, like a second actor making his entrance. Vossert was wearing a bathrobe too, and holding something like a scarf or a necktie taut between his hands. Apparently Mrs. Vossert wasn't aware that he was approaching her from the rear. At any rate, she didn't turn around. She just took another sip from her coffee cup as Vossert tiptoed up directly behind her. Still she didn't turn around or acknowledge his presence. He leaned toward her. In a flash, the scarf was around her neck and Vossert was yanking it tight.

Matt sucked in his breath with a wheeze as the scene before his eyes momentarily jiggled. What was this, some kind of joke? No, no joke. Mrs. Vossert's head jerked back and her legs shot out. Her coffee cup flew in the air, spilling coffee all over as Vossert twisted the scarf, the whole line of his body straining with the effort. Vossert was strangling her! Her hands reached up behind her and pulled at Vossert's hair, his arms, his robe.

Matt jumped up from behind Black Rock and in the jumping dropped his binoculars. He didn't even notice as they fell to the ground. He just took off and started back up the path at a run. The winter-tough briars and brambles grabbed at his jeans but he didn't notice that either. Unfortunately, Tebby must have thought he was playing some new game. Barking and yelping, she frisked at his heels so playfully, she almost tripped him up.

"Beat it, Tebby. Go home." His voice cracked with urgency.

For once Mrs. Shreve had left her front door unlocked. Matt stuck his head in as Tebby raced into the house past him. "Call the police, Mrs. Shreve. Quick! Vossert's killing his wife up at Bluff Cottage. Hurry!"

As soon as Matt saw by Mrs. Shreve's expression that she understood, he grabbed his bike from beside the garage where he had left it and pushed off. As he pedaled up Uncle Clement's Road toward the Vosserts', his heart was pumping as hard as his legs.

10

Matt was panting by the time he reached Bluff Cottage, but at least he wasn't totally breathless the way he was last time, and the hard push had warmed him up. He wiped his nose where it was dripping and started across the front yard. Halfway to the house, he stopped. Vossert was a strong-looking man with a thick-chested wrestler's kind of build. Young and tall didn't count much against that. Young and tall and out of shape, Matt amended. Hey, get on with it, he chided himself. This is no time for a debate.

Nevertheless, he pressed his ear up against the front door before doing anything drastic. The only sound from inside was the cheerful murmur of an early morning talk show. And with the front window shades pulled down, there was no way to see in. Matt tried the door. Locked.

"You in there, open up!" Matt punched the doorbell again and again, but there was no response.

"Let me in! Let me in!" Matt pounded the knocker until the trellises around the doorway rattled.

There was a sudden silence inside. Someone had turned off the TV. Vossert had heard all right, but obviously wasn't going to let Matt in. He'd have to try the back door. He raced down the driveway, around the side of the house to the back, but that door was locked too.

If only he could see in. Matt backed up as far as he could, to the edge of the drying yard where a tangle of blackberry vines was as prickly and dangerous as a snarl of barbed wire. Still he couldn't see in. The draperies across the sliding doors were closed now. Vossert had secured his little house into a fortress. In a frenzy of frustration, Matt scooped up a handful of pebbles from the drying yard and pitched them at the sliding doors.

"Let me in, you bastard!" The pebbles spattered against the glass before falling harmlessly to the deck.

That was when he heard it. The police siren. Matt ran around to the front yard just as Constable Hulse scrambled out of his cruiser. He left the motor running and the red roof light flashing as he hurried toward the house.

Constable Hulse grunted when he saw Matt. "You again, huh?"

"Quick, do something! Vossert killed his wife!"

The police radio crackled unintelligibly like the sur-realistic background to a surrealistic nightmare. Constable Hulse ran up the three narrow porch steps, followed by Matt. He stabbed the doorbell.

"East Tedham Police," he called out. "Open up, please." His breath puffed in little clouds.

"Break down the door! Shoot the lock open!" Now that help had arrived, Matt was on the verge of hysteria.

Constable Hulse didn't react or even look at Matt. "East Tedham Police. Open up." This time the command was louder and more authoritative.

Constable Hulse must have become aware of a presence on the other side of the door at the same time Matt did. They looked at each other as the latch clicked and the bolt was thrown back. When the door opened, Vossert, dressed in a bathrobe and pajamas, stood framed in the doorway, squinting and blinking as if he had just awakened and the bright morning sun hurt his eyes. "What is it?" he grumbled.

"We got a report of a possible assault. Can I come in?" Constable Hulse was polite but firm.

"What is this, some kind of joke? It isn't even seven o'clock. Of course you can't come in." Vossert started to close the door.

Vossert had killed his wife. Matt had seen the whole thing, and while he'd been running around trying to get in like a chicken with its head cut off, Vossert had probably hidden her body. But he wasn't going to get away with it. Matt grabbed Constable Hulse's arm.

"He killed his wife. He came up behind her and strangled her. I tell you I saw him do it." Matt's voice shot up about two octaves.

Vossert's dark eyebrows drew together in a furious line. "You saw me do what?"

Matt took an unconscious step back at the intensity of Vossert's anger. "I saw you . . . you . . . while your wife was watching TV I saw you . . . k . . . kill her . . ." Matt had wanted to sound resolute and forceful, but what came out was hesitant and squeaky.

Before Vossert could respond, Constable Hulse interrupted. "You realize what a serious accusation this is?"

"I saw the whole thing through binoculars. The draperies were open and I saw him do it. I swear I did." This time Matt's voice was steadier, though he was suddenly aware of how cold his hands and feet were. It was as if no blood were circulating in them at all.

Constable Hulse turned to Vossert. "I'd like to come inside."

"Not without a court order you can't."

"Then I'd like to speak to your wife."

"She's asleep, the same as I was."

"She's not asleep. I tell you he killed her!" Matt couldn't comprehend this ridiculous charade. Why didn't Constable Hulse just pull out his gun and force his way in?

Matt suddenly felt the full weight of Vossert's hand against his chest. "You get this straight, you little punk. I don't know what your problem is, drugs, booze or just plain crazy, but you go play your little games somewhere else. If you don't stop harassing my wife and me and spying on us through binoculars, I'll sign a complaint."

Vossert dropped his hand, but kept his fists balled as if he could hardly restrain himself from letting Matt have it. Matt's fists were clenched too. Who was Vossert to call him a punk when he'd just murdered his wife?

"I'm afraid, sir, I'll have to insist on entering . . ."

A movement in the open door cut Constable Hulse off in shocked midsentence. Matt momentarily went blank with shock himself. Mrs. Vossert had come up behind her husband and was standing in the doorway. Mrs. Vossert! Her hair was tousled and she was pulling on her bathrobe as if she had just gotten out of bed.

"What's all the commotion, Charles?" she asked, shivering.

Vossert put an arm around her shoulders. "Sorry we woke you up, Sidney, but apparently I'm being accused of killing you."

With a puzzled expression, Mrs. Vossert shook her head. "I don't understand."

There was a rushing in Matt's ears like waves crashing. All he could do was gape open-mouthed at Mrs. Vossert. It was like being a spectator at a play in which all the actors were speaking a foreign language.

"Our friend here," Vossert indicated Matt with a curt nod, "has accused me of killing you."

Mrs. Vossert tilted her head and looked from her husband to Matt back to her husband again. "What are you talking about?" She crossed her arms over her chest to warm herself.

"Are you Mrs. Vossert?" Constable Hulse sounded a little shaken himself.

"I've been Mrs. Vossert for eleven years so I guess I still am."

Constable Hulse turned to Matt, a look of anger tightening his narrow face. His weather-beaten cheeks had two bright spots of color. "Is this the woman you allegedly saw being killed?"

The question brought Matt up short. He wasn't watching a play. He was in it and he had better get his act together. Forcing himself to concentrate, he looked, really looked, at Mrs. Vossert. She was in her early thirties, tall, good-looking with blond hair, dressed in a soiled yellow bathrobe. Yes, this was the same woman he had been watching every day through his binoculars; the same woman he had sat next to in Dr. Grogan's office yesterday; the same woman he had just seen strangled by her husband. There was no doubt about it. Much as Matt wanted to say no, he couldn't.

His mouth and throat were so dry he had to swallow. "Yes."

"You're positive, real positive?" Constable Hulse pressed.

"Yes."

Constable Hulse's already thin mouth was a tight line. "Are you all right, Mrs. Vossert? Mebbe you'd consider coming to the station house with me."

"I certainly would not. This whole situation is ridiculous. Especially since I'm freezing out here." She turned and went back into the house.

"Then I'll be going . . ."

"No you won't, Hulse, not yet." Vossert pulled his bathrobe ties tight like a fighter preparing for a match.

"This is the second time you've annoyed my wife and me on some trumped-up charge. If I ever have any more trouble from you, I'll sue your town selectmen, the police department and you personally. And don't you forget it."

Without waiting for a reply. Vossert stepped back into his house and closed the door firmly behind him. Matt and Constable Hulse could hear the bolt shoot back in place and the latch click. The unintelligible voice from the police car radio that was still sputtering and snapping suddenly sounded very loud. A blue jay squawked somewhere overhead. Otherwise, silence.

"You heard what the man said, Runyon." Constable Hulse took off his hat and ran his hand over his bald spot. "You're making real problems, both for you and for me. You've gotten me out here twice for nothing and I'm warning you this had better be the last time." Despite the cold, Constable Hulse's forehead was beaded with sweat as he put his hat back on and headed across the yard toward his cruiser.

Matt's whole body started shivering and he didn't know if that was from the cold or from shock. As he watched Constable Hulse slam his cruiser into reverse and back out the driveway, he tried to put it together. Mrs. Vossert wasn't dead. She was alive and well and safe. And back in her house with her husband. The whole thing was over. But it couldn't be over. Matt had seen Vossert slip that scarf around her neck and strangle her. Her arms and legs had shot up in the air. Her coffee cup had spilled too, splashing coffee all over her.

Hey, that was right. Her coffee *had* splashed all over her. And when she had answered the door just now her yellow robe had been spotted with coffee stains. Wet coffee stains. If Mrs. Vossert had just woken up like she made out, there was no way her bathrobe could have been covered with fresh stains.

11

Matt didn't remember riding his bike from Bluff Cottage back to Mrs. Shreve's, but all of a sudden, there he was, on her front porch, still shivering. Before he could even ring the bell, she yanked the door open. Concern lined her face.

"It's okay, Mrs. Shreve. No one's been killed, or even hurt."

Matt's expression must have told her something too. She thumped her walker away from the door to let him in. "Bring in that plate of buns from the kitchen and get us both a cup of coffee, Matt, and you can tell me about it."

Matt didn't like coffee, but the bitter taste of it started his juices flowing again and he could feel his toes and fingers tingle as they came back to life. They sat in the parlor, Matt in the straightback Windsor chair that was so uncomfortable and Mrs. Shreve in her usual wing chair close to the warmth of the wood stove. Tebby lay almost on top of the stove too, half asleep. And they talked. At least Matt talked and Mrs. Shreve listened. He started with walking Tebby in the marsh and went right on through to noticing Mrs. Vossert's coffee-stained bathrobe. The whole time he was talking, he could tell by Mrs. Shreve's steady, straight gaze that she believed him, that she knew he hadn't been drunk or stoned or daydreaming or crazy. She wasn't even impatient when he went over it again trying to make some kind of sense of it all.

"You see," he tried to explain, "the Vosserts never open their draperies, not ever. It was like Vossert wanted me to see into his living room, as if the whole thing were an act set up just for me. I know he knows exactly what time I walk Tebby. I've even seen him watch me through binoculars. But he must have known I'd call the police and why would he want that?"

Mrs. Shreve shook her head. "I can't imagine what he . . ."

Matt didn't give her a chance to finish. "The Vosserts could have been playing some kind of kinky game, but they're not that kind of people. I even thought maybe Mrs. Vossert was just acting innocent because Vossert had threatened her, but if that were true, she'd have jumped at the chance to go to the station house with Constable Hulse when he asked her."

Matt took a long swallow of coffee and almost gagged. It was stone cold and horribly bitter. He quickly took a bite of his sweet bun to get rid of the taste. "What really bugs me is the way I come out the loser. Vossert really let me have it and so did Constable Hulse. It was just like the morning the Vosserts arrived when I thought there was a break-in. I looked bad on that one too."

Mrs. Shreve listened calmly, bending down from time to time to pet Tebby, whose golden sherry eyes were half open now as if she were listening. When Matt at last wound down, Mrs. Shreve leaned forward with an earnest expression. "What it's all about I can't fathom, Matt, but you did the right thing by calling the police whether anyone believes you or not. You can live with that and that's what matters in the end." She reached for her walker and with effort stood up. "Now if you don't mind, I'm going back to bed. I spent a fitful night and I'm tired."

It was only then that Matt realized Mrs. Shreve was still in her bathrobe and slippers. Ordinarily she was fully dressed no matter how early in the morning he showed up to walk Tebby. And she did look tired. Dark circles framed her eyes.

"Hey, I'm sorry, Mrs. Shreve. I'd better get going."

When she didn't argue, he got his things together and said good-bye. He hated to leave. Although Mrs. Shreve had hardly said a word, she had listened and had never once put him down or doubted his story. Her acceptance always left Matt feeling a lot less angry around the edges.

But where to go now? He couldn't face school, but he didn't want to go home to an empty house either. And if he rode his bike around, Constable Hulse would probably pick him up on some phony charge like truancy or loitering.

That was how he ended up on the beach, his last resort. Fortunately, a warming southerly breeze had blown the early morning cold out to sea, leaving puff-clouds maneuvering and jostling in a flag-blue sky with the fresh smell of the salt water tangy and crisp enough to taste. Although gulls circled and gyrated overhead making a terrible racket, today Matt didn't mind their squabbling. They somehow reminded him of the way he and Bucky wrestled and horsed around as the only way they knew of expressing their affection.

Matt sat down back by the dunes where he was protected from the wind, clasped his knees up close to his chest to stay warm and scanned the shoreline. Actually, there wasn't much to see. Two fishermen in high boots were surf casting down the beach a way. A couple of freighters steamed across the horizon and an occasional small fishing boat cruised past, but because that was the extent of the action, Matt ended up watching the surf.

Today the water sparkled deep cobalt, with the white caps flashes of quicksilver in the sun. The breakers, cresting and curling, formed a good distance out, where they hung suspended before crashing in a fury of white foam that fanned out the length of the beach. Sucked out to sea with a slurp, they joined the next breaking roller to slap on the beach again. Swell, curl, break, hiss. Each wave was endlessly the same and yet infinitely different. Swell, curl, break, hiss . . . swell, curl, break, hiss . . . the hypnotic pounding was soothing in a way that Matt didn't even try to understand. His mind emptied and drained of everything but the rhythm. Swell, curl, break, hiss . . . swell, curl, break, hiss . . .

All of a sudden he felt the sting of sharp sand pepper his face. And he was cold. He must have fallen asleep. As he stretched stiffly, he realized his jeans were damp through. The wind had shifted again so that it now whipped off the water with a piercing bite. The ocean looked different too, calmer, quieter, rippling over suddenly exposed sandbars as the tide began its retreat. Slip, slap, slip, slap. The waves were a pale imitation of their earlier fury. Matt jammed his hands into his pockets to warm them and looked for the fishermen down the beach. They were gone. It was time to go home.

As soon as he pulled into the driveway, he saw his mother's Plymouth and when he opened the front door, he heard her calling.

"Is that you, Matt? Come upstairs, please."

To his surprise, Matt found his mother in his and Bucky's room packing Bucky's duffle bag. She was dressed in her one good suit and her hair was carefully brushed feathery instead of combed in its usual slapdash style. She barely glanced up.

"Bucky and I are driving to Boston for a seven o'clock

flight, Matt," she announced without any preliminaries. "We have to be in Denver by tomorrow. Warren is trying to ram this custody thing through." Her voice sounded strained and she looked strained too. "I'd like you to pick up Bucky at Cub Scouts. You don't have to tell him what it's all about. Just say . . . oh, I don't know . . . just say anything."

But that was terrible. In the back of his mind Matt had been hoping this whole thing with Bucky would blow over. "Does Bucky have to go with you?"

His mother's nod was tight. "Bucky's considered to be of the age of reason and the judge wants him there in person to help decide his own future. I hate to put him through it, but I have no choice. Anyway, go and get him, will you?"

"I'll be here in the house alone." It wasn't a question.

"I could ask Amy Melcher to come and stay with you."

"No-thank-you." Emphatically no. Amy Melcher worked on the newspaper with Mom and was a nonstop smoker and a nonstop talker who would drive him crazy. Besides, being alone might work out okay, especially since spring vacation started next week. He could get up when he wanted, do what he wanted, and . . . but wait a minute. He wouldn't have a car.

"Can't I drive you to Boston, Mom?" As Matt waited for her reply, he pulled out a pair of dry jeans and jockey shorts from his dresser.

For the first time, his mother managed a smile. "Thanks for the offer, Matt, but I've been having clutch trouble and I'd just as soon you didn't drive while I'm gone. Besides, we'll need a car to get home from the airport. And you can manage without a car. Pettingill's Market delivers and . . . say, I almost forgot. Pettingill's reminds me I've got good news for you."

68

Not much good news had come his way lately. "Like what?"

"Like Dr. Grogan called today to say your last blood test was so improved you can resume all normal activities including an after-school job. And just today Pettingill's Market sent in an ad for a part-time driver. I shouldn't have done it but I delayed the ad to give you a chance to check into it."

"Hey, thanks, Mom. That's great."

That really was good news. Matt had held such high hopes for his last blood test, he hadn't even let himself think about this latest one. And a possible job waiting for him. Wow! Buying a Ruger 77 rifle and hunting in Colorado suddenly became a possibility again. Maybe if he got started right now, he could stop at Pettingill's on the way to pick up Bucky. If there wasn't time for an interview, he could at least fill out an application. He raced into the bathroom and changed into his dry clothes.

As it turned out, he didn't need an application. Old Mr. Pettingill knew all about him, or at least about his family. "So you're the Hecker boy, are you? I knew your grandparents, Maude and John Hecker, real well. Fine folks. Maude's father built the Folger house out on Featherbed Lane . . ." On and on he rambled about the Hecker family history. Matt didn't care. Mr. Pettingill could talk about the Heckers all day long if it would get him the job. Apparently it did. At least Mr. Pettingill hired him on the spot.

As soon as Bucky got cleaned up and changed, he and his mother took off, Mom wearing unaccustomed earrings and makeup, trying to look cheerful, and Bucky not even having to try because he didn't know yet why they were going. All he could think about was seeing his father again and all his old friends. As they pulled out of the driveway and Matt saw Bucky's wide toothless grin and blond hair all slicked down, he felt a terrible wrench. If Warren won

69

the custody suit, Bucky might not come back to East Tedham at all. But Warren couldn't win the suit. Bucky needed Mom and Matt . . . and they needed Bucky.

Matt felt really down going back into the empty house. It was a small house, just a summer cottage really, converted for year-round living. He wandered from room to room, picking up a magazine and putting it down, looking at his mother's paperweight collection as if he had never seen it before, plucking dead leaves off the spider plant. And the whole time, his stomach was growling. Hey, food. Maybe food would make him feel better. He hadn't eaten since breakfast.

He got out a bowl of cold spaghetti, threw it in a pot and turned the gas up high. As he watched the spaghetti sputter and spit, he suddenly realized he hadn't told his mother about what had happened at Bluff Cottage that morning. Mom and Bucky leaving and his new job had all been so immediate; the Vosserts, Constable Hulse, his talk with Mrs. Shreve, and even his hours on the beach seemed as remote as if they had happened a hundred years ago.

12

Being alone worked out better than Matt had expected, and the job was good too. It was great to have wheels under him, even if it was only a beat-up ten-year-old jeep pickup. The routine was easy. The after-school bus let him off in town and when he got to Pettingill's, the groceries were packed and waiting for him to deliver. With the help of a local street map, plus trial and error, he found his way around the Tedhams pretty well. He already knew East Tedham's twisting narrow roads. Tedham proper was the business district—mostly stores and shops clustered around the village green topped by the big white Colonial church like icing on a cake. North Tedham was all country elegance, large old homes half hidden behind high shrubbery and ancient trees.

On Matt's third day out, he reached the end of his list early. "Beach Plum," No Name Lane, North Tedham, was his last delivery. No Name Lane. That was a new one, even for Cape Cod. But when Matt turned onto it, he realized it was probably called No Name because it was just a narrow little dirt road. Dirt road or not, as Matt passed imposing stone gateposts, manicured lawns and huge homes discreetly set back from the street, he was aware that No Name Lane, North Tedham, was *the* address to have. And when he reached the end of the road, he saw that "Beach Plum" was *the* house on No Name Lane.

A couple of acres of lawn bordered a large white rambling Victorian mansion complete with porches, verandas and cupolas which perched in lonely splendor on a cliff overlooking the full sweep of the Atlantic Ocean, like a grande dame surveying her domain. As Matt drove up the dazzling white crushed-shell driveway, he noticed a tennis court to his right and a big barn to his left with a Land Rover, a Mercedes 330L and a Volvo wagon parked inside, like the interior of some foreign car agency.

When Matt rang the back doorbell, he expected a butler, or at the very least a maid, to answer. So when Julie Chamberlain opened the door, he was stunned. His first reaction was, What is she doing here? His second reaction was she was here because she probably lived here. Matt wasn't angry at Julie any more, but he didn't go out of his way for her either. He ran into her on and off in school, but she was always headed somewhere in a hurry or surrounded by her Muir Club satellites. Now here she was. Alone.

"Hi, Matt," she greeted him. "When I heard Mom ordering groceries from Pettingill's, I figured you'd be delivering them. Come on in."

All of a sudden, Matt felt like a fool. He was wearing the kelly green jacket with the Pettingill's Market patch on the pocket that Mr. Pettingill made all his employees wear, and the market pickup parked in the drive behind him was a heap of junk. Not that Julie looked that great herself. She wore an old sweatshirt, faded jeans and ripped running shoes. Nevertheless, as she held the door open for him to carry in the groceries, Matt could feel the back of his scalp begin to prickle.

"How did you know I delivered for Pettingill's?" he

asked, though he didn't know why he bothered. Around here, no one's business was private.

Julie must have thought the question wasn't worth answering either. "You were really lucky to get a job," she said instead. "Out-of-season jobs are impossible to find."

As if you'd ever need one, Matt thought, glancing around the enormous kitchen and pantry. Although all the appliances were shiny new, they were designed to look old-fashioned. A huge refrigerator was made up like an old ice-box, a range with eight burners faked it as an antique wood stove and the rustic looking counters and cabinets were all Formica. The phony bit was especially annoying when Matt compared it to his mother's tiny kitchen which not only looked like a dated 1940s kitchen, but was a dated 1940s kitchen.

As Matt set the groceries down on the butcher block table, he noticed a dollar bill with a note clipped to it that Julie's mother must have left. "Tip for Pettingill's boy," it read.

Matt picked it up. "Shall I take this now or are you going to slip it in my pocket?" He hated the resentment in his voice but there it was, out before he could do anything about it.

Julie looked startled. Then angry. "You can stuff it in your ear for all I care."

Matt was sure she didn't think he'd take it, so he stuck it in his pocket, note and all. "Thank you. Pettingill's-boy is plumb grateful for the Beach Plum tip."

Julie abruptly turned her back and started to unpack the groceries, slamming them down on the counter so hard her long hair bounced. "Take it or leave it. Nobody's forcing you to do anything, including being halfway civil."

Matt hesitated. Her back was to him so he didn't have to confront her face to face. It was the perfect opportunity to say something to cool things off. Then he noticed a little alligator stitched on the hip of her blue jeans. Designer jeans. Her faded jeans were as phony as her kitchen. Matt didn't even say good-bye. He just left, slamming the door behind him.

As he climbed back in the pickup, he felt as if the top of his head were about to blow off and he didn't know if he was madder at Julie or himself. He started the motor and backed up faster than he should have.

"Matt, hey, Matt." It was Julie on her back porch waving to him.

Matt braked but didn't turn off the motor as she ran down the driveway toward him.

"Have you got a couple of minutes?" she asked as soon as she'd caught up to him.

Although Matt had finished his deliveries and wasn't due back at Pettingill's for another half hour, he glanced at his watch and frowned. "Yeah, but just a few." He pointedly left the motor running as he climbed out.

Julie stuck her hands in her pockets and looked Matt straight in the eye. "Every time we meet, we tee off on each other. It's dumb. I mean, I certainly don't have anything against you if that's what you think. In fact, I . . . I like you. So what gives?"

There was so much Matt wanted to say. How she had it all together and had friends and a slot in school and money and knew how to be her own person, and he was just hanging onto the fringes with his fingertips. But he didn't say any of it. "I guess I can't stand your chewing gum for one thing." Matt took a deep breath. "And tell me how you'd feel if I tipped you a dollar?"

Before answering, Julie shoved her gum to one side of her mouth. "Do Pettingill's other customers tip you?" she asked instead of answering.

Julie's face glowed pink from the wind and she was smiling a sudden impish smile. Her teeth were small and white and even, except where one of her front teeth overlapped the other a little. It was just crooked enough, like her nose, to be appealing. Without meaning to, Matt smiled back, and in the smiling, the whole tight core of him loosened and relaxed. Sheepishly, he reached in his pocket for his wallet and took out a handful of bills and change. He already knew what his day's tips amounted to, $13.50.

When Julie saw the fistful of money, she laughed. And the tension instantly eased between them. Matt leaned back into the pickup and turned off the ignition. "You've got some house here," he said in an attempt to start their conversation from scratch.

"It was built in the Year One. I've never lived anywhere else. The only thing that ever changes around here is the cast of characters." This time Julie was the one who sounded resentful.

"What do you mean?"

Without discussing it, they had both started walking across the yard toward the cliff.

"I mean it's always been Mom's house and Mom's money and only her husbands change." Julie kicked a stone ahead of her on the path.

"Your mother's remarried?" Dumb. What else could she mean?

"Mom's on husband number four." Julie sounded defiant, and looked defiant, as if daring Matt to say anything. He had to give her credit for telling him at all. She could have let him go on thinking that she lived in some kind of sugar-coated wonderland. If nothing else, it certainly put them on a more equal footing.

Still, fair was fair. "My mother's divorced too," Matt volunteered. "My dad died when I was a kid and Mom remarried. But it didn't work out so here we are back on Cape Cod where Mom used to spend her summers. Unfortunately."

Julie's gray-green eyes were sympathetic. "You know, the high school really isn't so bad and the kids are okay too. As far as I'm concerned, it's a hundred percent better than

75

my other alternative. Mom wanted me to go to boarding school, but I absolutely refused. Now Mom apologizes to all her friends because she's got a daughter who goes to a public high school. Mom's own private tragedy." Julie gave a short laugh.

For all her house and cars and money, Julie was okay. More than okay. Gutsy. She told it the way it was and didn't pull any punches.

"That is some spectacular view," Matt said and he meant it. They had reached the rail fence that bordered the edge of the cliff, a good sixty feet above the water, with the coastline stretching for miles in either direction. A rambling ribbon of white spray separated the amber beach and the dark blue of the sea. Tiny distant gulls skimmed the water like scraps of cotton. Today the ocean looked navy blue and Matt wondered if the color actually changed or just appeared to.

"See, Matt, there's the ORV trail the Muir Club is trying to do something about."

"What's ORV?"

"The off-road vehicle trail. You know, for four-wheel drives like dune buggies and jeeps and pickups."

Matt looked south where Julie was pointing. At first he saw only a little yellow beach house, accessible from the cliff by a zig-zag erector set of steps. And then he saw the trail. Two wide tracks ran parallel to the ocean between the sand dunes and the brown spikes of winter beach grass.

"You can see from here there isn't a stalk of grass left anywhere near the trail." Julie was back on her soapbox. "Without those six-foot-deep beach grass roots to hold the sand, the ocean will sweep right in and take over the dunes."

For once Matt didn't jump in and say what he thought, that the ORV trail looked like fun and he'd love to drive it. Instead he pointed to a distant boat and asked what it was. That subject led to sailing and to parents and divorce and then onto Matt moving and Matt missing Colorado and Matt being sick with mono. Mostly, it seemed, they talked about Matt. Matt knew how boring he probably sounded, but Julie acted interested enough for him to keep going.

"It's not that I'm such a great skier, but I used to go almost every weekend and I miss it." Matt propped his elbows on the fence and watched a tiny toy tanker steam across the distant horizon.

"Dad has a place near Sugarbush and he lets me have kids up to ski over Christmas vacation." Julie leaned against the railing too.

"You're kidding! There's skiing around here?" In his excitement, Matt spun around and as he did, he brushed against Julie. He pulled away, but he could tell by the way she turned toward him that she was aware of his touch.

"Sugarbush is in Vermont, but it's not too bad a drive."

Matt suddenly realized the tanker was fading out of sight in a darkening sky. "Hey, it's late. I gotta go." If he didn't get the pickup back, Mr. Pettingill would have his neck.

While he and Julie had been talking, Matt had noticed an access road leading onto the ORV trail right below where they were standing. How could he resist trying it? The trail looked like a more direct way back into town, plus in the old pickup it would be a real challenge.

As soon as he reached the ORV trail, he looked back up toward the cliff to check if Julie was still there. Good, she'd gone. Not that he was trying to put anything over on her, but there was no reason for her to get all whipped up just because he wanted a little adventure. He and Julie had arrived at some kind of truce and though it wasn't anything spectacular, he didn't want to spoil it.

The trail made for more difficult driving than he had

anticipated. The sand was looser and the ruts deeper than they had appeared from the cliff above. The pickup pitched and yawed and even stalled a couple of times, but somehow he kept the old heap going, even when the tires spun out. One thing for sure, it wasn't any short cut into town. After two miles, he wasn't even certain where he was.

But half a mile later, he suddenly spotted Nimicut Salt Marsh in the distance. He hiked up in his seat to orient himself, and to his surprise, saw the Vosserts' house almost directly to his right, sitting on its lonely little bluff. But why should that be a surprise? Bluff Cottage was directly north of the marsh. Stunted scrub oaks hid Matt from view, though he could see the house clearly. And on this side, the draperies were open and the shades up. The Vosserts must not know there was an access to their house from the north.

Matt couldn't have explained why, but a quick stab of excitement raced through him. The knowledge of this approach from the north was like a new-found treasure, known only to him.

13

Matt's good mood lasted right through to the next morning, and it wasn't just the new back way to the Vosserts' he was thinking about as he biked to Mrs. Shreve's, but Julie too. He pictured her slightly crooked smile and the way she'd unobtrusively gotten rid of her chewing gum and he saw some kind of future possibilities. Hey, didn't she say she jogged on the beach every day? With the sun rising in a thin blue sky and not a breath of wind for once, it was a perfect day for jogging. He'd take Tebby to the beach and see if he could find her.

But out of habit, as soon as Matt reached Black Rock, he released Tebby and she took off. Matt watched her go. Her long body seemed almost disjointed, as if her hips and rear legs worked separately from the rest of her. Smooth, that was what Tebby was, a smooth jet black streak, built for running, swimming, retrieving. She was built even better than Dad's spaniel Sarge who had died of old age three years ago. If she was trained, she'd make a great bird dog, no doubt about it.

Lately Tebby had made a beeline for the far side of

the marsh, digging and sniffing around between a pair of pitch pine trees, and that was where she was headed now. Matt didn't like it. Those trees were on the edge of the marsh only a little way down from Bluff Cottage and Matt had had enough of tangling with the Vosserts.

"Come on, girl! Here, Tebby!" Matt whistled through his teeth, something he had just learned to do and to which she usually responded. Now her ears pricked up, she cocked her head at Matt, then she went right back to her digging. She must be after some animal over there, though Matt was sure it wasn't the fox. He's seen the fox once or twice lately, but always at the other end of the marsh, nowhere near where Tebby was scavenging now.

Matt was getting impatient. That dog badly needed discipline. "Tebby, come here! Tebby!"

She must have sensed his displeasure, because this time she loped in Matt's direction, her strong legs eating up the distance between them. He clipped on her leash. "Bad girl. You stay away from there. C'mon now, let's get going." At this rate, they'd never find Julie.

The only way Matt had ever approached the beach before was by the public access road. Now he pulled Tebby along a little trail around the mucky fringes of the marsh. As they made their way past a gnarled cedar tree, they inadvertently flushed out a great blue heron. Matt didn't know who was the most startled, the bird, Tebby or he. Certainly he and Tebby jumped as the heron gave a low-pitched croak and took off right in front of them with a flapping of its heavy wings. What a strange bird, both graceful and awkward, Matt thought as he watched it slowly gain altitude, its long sharp bill like a blackboard pointer and its sticklike legs trailing behind like a rudder. Matt raised his imaginary Ruger 77 to his shoulder and lined up the heron in his sights. Forget it. An easy target like that wouldn't even be sportsmanlike.

And then he and Tebby were on the rickety old bridge that crossed over the sluice dam. In some ancient time, a dam had been constructed here to control the amount of water that flowed into the marsh from the ocean. Now the eight-foot-wide sluice gates were permanently open so that only the rising and falling of the tides regulated the flow of water.

It was high tide now, really high. The wide channels that meandered through the sand dunes from the sea funneled under the bridge through the sluice and cascaded into the marsh in a roaring waterfall. Matt leaned over the bridge railing and dropped a stick in the water. It was immediately sucked out of sight in the turbulence, a moment later bobbing up thirty feet away. The thundering force of the water swirled it around and around until it floated out of sight. It was amazing that the placid little tidal creeks that looped though the salt marsh originated in this tremendous burst of power.

Tebby whined and pulled on her leash.

"You're right, Tebs, let's go," Matt agreed.

They crossed the bridge and followed a path through the stiff brown beach grass toward the dunes. At the top of the highest dune, Matt checked in either direction for Julie, but she was nowhere in sight. He and Tebby must have wasted too much time. With the warming sun on his face, he lingered a moment, watching a flock of sandpipers play tag with the surf, their little pipe-cleaner legs scurrying them back to safety every time a wave stretched toward them.

He'd better be heading back. Ever since Bucky and his mother had been gone, Matt had been eating breakfast with Mrs. Shreve. The smell of coffee brewing and bacon frying always greeted him when he returned with Tebby. But today the house smelled cold and blank.

"Mrs. Shreve?"

"I'm in here, Matt," Mrs. Shreve called from her bedroom. Her usually crisp voice sounded thin.

Matt went to her bedroom door and called through. "Are you okay?"

"I'm not feeling too fit this morning, Matt, so I'm going to rest a bit. I daresay you'll have to make your own breakfast."

"No problem." Matt hesitated. Knowing how independent Mrs. Shreve was, he hated to interfere. On the other hand, maybe she needed help. "Is there anything I can do? Do you want me to call the doctor?"

He could hear Mrs. Shreve's "humph" through the door. "No indeed. I'll be fine."

As Matt left, he resolved to check in on her later when he was making his deliveries. And that afternoon, when he went over his list, he was pleased to see he'd be making a delivery not far from her house at #38 Uncle Clement's Road.

There weren't many houses on Uncle Clement's Road, and as Matt drove up the hill, it began to register on him in a very unpleasant way that #38 might turn out to be the Vosserts'. It was. Now how was he supposed to handle this? Carefully, he decided, as he shifted into first and drove slowly down their driveway. At least their Cadillac wasn't in the garage. If they weren't home, he'd just leave the groceries on the back porch, even though Mr. Pettingill had expressly told him never to do that.

His speculation was a waste of time. Mrs. Vossert opened the back door almost as soon as he knocked.

"Groceries from Pettingill's." Matt's voice was as reedy as a child's.

Mrs. Vossert must not have seen beyond the green Pettingill's jacket. She opened the door and waved him in. "Put them on the table," she ordered as she picked up her pocketbook from the counter. She tried to open it to get out a tip, but the clasp was stuck.

"Damn," she whispered under her breath as she struggled with it.

Matt didn't even want a tip. All he wanted was to get out. "That's okay, Mrs. Vossert, forget it," he assured her.

Right away he realized the "Mrs. Vossert" was a mistake. Her head jerked up and she looked Matt in the face for the first time. She blinked hard as if she couldn't believe what she was seeing. "What are you doing here?"

She made it sound as if he'd done something terrible. "I work for Pettingill's."

"Since when?"

"I started Monday."

"My husband told you never to show your face around here again." Furious, she took a step forward, raising her pocketbook almost threateningly. She was nearly as tall as he was, though what she could do to him, Matt couldn't imagine. Nevertheless he retreated a step.

Her hands. It was as if her hands were lit by an electric current. Her poison ivy was all cleared up now so that her rings and jewelry were back on and her hands looked perfectly normal. But that must have been what was bothering him all along. Her hands shouldn't have looked normal. When Matt first met Mrs. Vossert that morning she had arrived, the middle finger on her right hand had been partly missing. Matt remembered wondering if she'd had an accident or been born that way. Now the finger was as normal as his.

His eyes slid from Mrs. Vossert's hands to her face. She was watching him study her hands and she was clearly alarmed. Slowly, as if she didn't want to attract any more attention to them than she already had, she lowered her pocketbook to the table and clenched her fists.

"Well, what are you waiting for?" she snapped.

"Nothing . . . I'm going . . ." As Matt backed up

toward the door, his heart was beating so hard, the Pettingill's Market patch on his pocket rose and fell with its rhythm.

Matt walked down the back porch stairs as normally as he could just in case Mrs. Vossert was watching. He even tried to whistle as he climbed in the pickup and backed out the driveway. But whistling wasn't possible. All that came out were a few breathy wheezes.

This was incredible . . . weird . . . Matt couldn't even put a word to it. This woman was the same Mrs. Vossert he had been watching all these weeks through binoculars, he knew that. He also knew that it was the same Mrs. Vossert who had sat next to him in Dr. Grogan's office, and the same Mrs. Vossert who had acted out that murder scene. But it definitely was not the same Mrs. Vossert he had met the day the Vosserts first arrived in East Tedham.

Matt paused at the end of the Vosserts' driveway, trying to recall what that first Mrs. Vossert had looked like. How her voice had sounded. What color her hair had been. But he couldn't. She had been wearing smoked glasses and a scarf had covered her hair. As to her voice, they hadn't exchanged more than ten words so that was no help either. All he could remember about her was her expensive jewelry and her partly missing finger.

Screech! Honk!

Matt had pulled out of the driveway without looking and almost hit a car coming in the other direction. Wow, he had better pull himself together or, Mrs. Vossert or no Mrs. Vossert, he'd end up totaled and so would Pettingill's pickup.

14

Matt had already passed Mrs. Shreve's house when he remembered he had planned to check in on her. He jammed on the brakes and backed up. Mrs. Shreve would help him. She'd be willing to listen and maybe she'd have some idea as to what was going on. He liked her down-to-earth way of looking at things that cut to the heart. Right now he could use a little of that because he wasn't capable of cutting through to anything.

But when he turned in her driveway, another car was already there, a Ford with MD plates. Mrs. Shreve didn't believe in doctors. When she broke her ankle, she'd told Matt it was the first time she had seen a doctor in fifteen years. Now an MD car was parked right in her driveway.

Matt pushed open the unlocked front door. "Mrs. Shreve?" Tentative. Concerned.

At the sound of his voice, Tebby came bounding in from the direction of Mrs. Shreve's bedroom and leapt on him, almost knocking him over in her enthusiasm for the walk she anticipated. Distracted, he pushed her down. "Mrs. Shreve?" Louder this time.

"Yes?" It was a man's voice in reply and a moment

later, Dr. Grogan came striding down the hall. He was frowning as he made notes on a pad of paper.

"Hello, Dr. Grogan," Matt greeted him. "How's Mrs. Shreve?"

Dr. Grogan finished whatever he was writing and looked up. "Oh, hello, there, Matthew."

"How is Mrs. Shreve, Dr. Grogan?"

"I don't know and won't know until we do some tests." Dr. Grogan slipped the pad of paper into his pocket. "Emily is complaining of chest pains so in spite of her strenuous objections, I'm putting her in the hospital. Now I want to get in touch with her daughter Donna in Wisconsin, also in spite of Emily's strenuous objections, I might add. Do you know where the phone is?"

Matt pointed to the phone that Mrs. Shreve kept tucked in the corner of her cherry desk. "Is it okay if I go see her?" he asked.

At Dr. Grogan's nod, Matt headed back to Mrs. Shreve's bedroom with Tebby right beside him, her nails clicking on the bare floorboards.

"Mrs. Shreve? It's me, Matt."

"Come in." Her voice was even weaker than it had been that morning and when Matt went in her appearance was a shock too. Looking tiny and frail, she was propped up in a big four-poster bed that seemed to swallow her up. Her cast was an awkward mound under a faded patchwork quilt.

"Douglas Grogan is putting me in the hospital. Can you imagine anything so foolish?" she whispered. "I've never been in a hospital in my life." Her words ran together as if her tongue didn't work right, and as she spoke, Matt realized one of the reasons she looked so frail and vulnerable was because she wasn't wearing her false teeth. It was as unsettling as if he had seen her naked, and he looked away.

"You'll be better off in the hospital, Mrs. Shreve. And

you'll be home soon," he reassured her. As if he knew anything about it.

"I'm concerned about Tebby."

Tebby had come up beside Matt and now, at the sound of her name, nuzzled her wide black nose into the covers as if to nudge her mistress out of bed. She was whimpering, obviously aware that something was wrong, but not sure what. Even her hazel eyes looked sad. Matt patted her silky head. "I'll take her home with me. Now that I'm alone in the house Tebby will be good company."

"Thank you, Matt. Her food is in the pantry . . ." Mrs. Shreve's voice faded away, her eyes closed, and Matt thought she'd fallen asleep. Then her blue-veined eyelids flickered open. "Feed her twice a day and she needs a bath and a brushing. I haven't been able to . . ." Her words trailed off and her eyes closed again.

"Matthew." Dr. Grogan signaled from the hall. "I gave Emily a shot to let her get some sleep," he said as he walked Matt to the front door. "I just got in touch with Donna and she's flying in tomorrow. Everything's under control but the dog." He made it sound like a question.

Why didn't he just come out and ask Matt to take Tebby instead of beating around the bush? "I already told Mrs. Shreve I'd take Tebby."

Dr. Grogan nodded his approval. "By the way, how are you feeling?"

"Good." All of a sudden Matt realized he was good. Not terrific, but getting there. He grinned. "I'm doing fine."

Dr. Grogan clapped him on the back. "Glad to hear it. Now I'll wait here for the ambulance."

Though it was a clear dismissal, Matt stood his ground. "Is Mrs. Shreve going to be all right?"

But Dr. Grogan wouldn't commit himself. "We'll just have to wait for the tests. That is, if I can keep her in the

87

hospital. When she broke her ankle, I wanted her to stay at the Sea View Rest Home to recuperate but you can imagine how she took that suggestion." Dr. Grogan smiled ruefully and Matt had to smile too. He couldn't picture Mrs. Shreve staying anywhere that was called the Sea View Rest Home.

Tebby jumped right into the pickup with Matt and sat up in the passenger seat as if she'd been riding with him all her life. Matt reached over and stroked her, raising a flurry of dust, hair and dandruff. She really did need a bath and a brushing. But that would have to wait for the weekend. Right now, fond of her as he was, Tebby was going to be a complication. It would be easy to walk her before school, but with his new job, he didn't get home at night until after six. Well, maybe Mrs. Shreve wouldn't be in the hospital long. No, of course she wouldn't. She'd be okay soon. She had to be.

That night, after walking and feeding Tebby, fixing dinner, studying for an English test and unsuccessfully trying to repair the back door lock, Matt was in bed before he even had a chance to think about that other complication in his life, Mrs. Vossert, or whoever she was.

Mrs. Vossert. At least she called herself Mrs. Vossert. But then so had that woman he had met the first day the Vosserts had arrived. Maybe they were both Mrs. Vossert, the first one divorced and gone, and the second one a new wife. But it wasn't that simple. Matt distinctly remembered Vossert calling her Sidney that first morning because at the time he had thought it was a strange name for a woman. And in Dr. Grogan's office Vossert had called this second woman Sidney too. There was no way Vossert could have married two women both named Sidney. Besides, they wore the same diamond wristwatch and elaborate rings. Only their hands were different.

There was something else. When Mrs. Vossert had reappeared that day out on the deck after she hadn't been around for a week or so, Matt's gut reaction had been that it wasn't the same woman he had first met. Her size, shape and whole appearance had seemed different. So no matter which way he sliced it, he still came up with two separate women, both calling themselves Mrs. Vossert and both answering to the name Sidney. Somehow it was all tied up with that weird strangling act . . .

Vroom! A black shadow rocketed across the room, landing on top of Matt with an impact that almost knocked him out of bed. A yell strangled in his throat as he struggled against the stifling weight. An intruder! Vossert! Out to kill him! Help! Matt rolled over trying to get out of bed, but he was pinned down. And then it barked. It was Tebby. He had forgotten all about her. Matt's heartbeat filled his whole chest as Tebby's tail enthusiastically thumped against the covers.

Not only was it after midnight before Matt finally fell asleep, but it was before dawn when Tebby woke him up. Matt glanced at his digital clock in the dark. 5:18. And Tebby was raring to go, pawing at the blankets, her golden eyes bright. By her energy level, Matt figured this was the time she got started every morning. Knowing Mrs. Shreve, it probably was. And there was no quieting her down. She pulled at Matt's T-shirt sleeve with her teeth, then ran to the door and back again, barking for him to get up. Matt groaned and pushed the covers off. He might as well get up. With Tebby around, sleeping was out. At least with an early start, he'd be more likely to find Julie on the beach.

As he got dressed, he realized how much he needed to find Julie. He had spent half the night turning his brain inside out and upside down puzzling over the Vosserts with no success. He just had to talk everything over with someone and Julie was the only one around.

This was one morning when he wasn't going to let Tebby off her leash in the marsh, no matter how she whined. Sure enough, as soon as they got to Black Rock, she tugged and strained to be let go and it took every bit of Matt's strength to pull her along the path. And all the while she was looking over toward the two pitch pine trees on the far side of the marsh. There was certainly something over there attracting her, but Matt saw no sign of an animal hole or nest or anything but a lot of loose dirt where Tebby had been digging.

Digging. But that was exactly the spot where Vossert had been digging the afternoon Matt had seen him with a pick and shovel. Vossert had tamped down the soil between those two pine trees with the back of his shovel before putting the pick and shovel over his shoulder and going back into his house.

But nothing was growing there, no plants, no shrubs, no ground cover. Nothing at all to arouse Tebby. Unless . . . unless . . . Vossert had been planting something else there . . . burying something . . . or someone . . . a someone who was missing . . .

Matt didn't even want to put what was ricocheting around his head into anything as tangible as words. Instead he just stood and stared at the loose patch of dug-up soil on the far side of Nimicut Salt Marsh before towing Tebby along the path on his way to find Julie.

15

*T*he wind was sharp and biting out of the northwest, whipping up Lilliputian sand storms, stinging Matt's ankles, leveling footprints and animal tracks. White caps danced across a choppy sea. No one would run on the beach on a day like this. No one but Julie. There she was, a hundred yards or so down the beach jogging along into the wind.

"Julie, hey, Julie! Wait for me!" The wind snatched up Matt's words and flung them away.

Luckily Tebby had seen Julie too and took off after her. At the feel of Tebby's cold wet nose against her hand, Julie stopped and turned around. When she saw Matt, she waited for him to catch up to her. But running into the wind was hard work. Despite his assurances to Dr. Grogan about feeling great, Matt realized he was still in terrible shape.

Julie, who was jogging in place while she waited, was laughing by the time he reached her. "You look like you're on the last leg of the Boston Marathon." She didn't even sound winded.

"Julie . . . I've got to talk to you . . . now . . ."
Matt's chest was heaving.

"About what?"

"You won't believe . . ." That was no way to begin.
"You remember the Vosserts, those people who live in
Bluff Cottage opposite the marsh?" Matt paused to snatch
a couple of deep breaths. "Well, today it suddenly hit me
that Vossert's been . . . say, can't you stand still? The
way you're bobbing up and down I might as well be talking
to a jackhammer."

"I'm all warmed up and don't want to cool down."
Julie must have sensed his annoyance because there was an
edge to her voice too.

Oh no, not again, Matt groaned to himself. They just
couldn't get into an argument now, not when he needed to
talk to Julie so badly. He forced himself to play it cool.
"Why don't we just keep walking? You'd stay warmed up
that way, wouldn't you?" Matt even managed to sound
pleasant, though he was still panting and breathless.

Julie shrugged and started out, setting a brisk pace.
Tebby was long since gone, after the gulls, into the water,
curiously nosing an old horseshoe crab shell. Absent-
mindedly, Matt picked up a stick, heaved it for her to fetch
and she took off after it like a shot. Fetching was what she
liked to do best in all the world.

"Well?" Julie's nose was red, with a little drip on the
end of it Matt was sure she didn't know was there.

"It's about the Vosserts. I found out something that
blew my mind," Matt began again. "When I saw Mrs. Vossert yesterday, I realized that she isn't the same Mrs. Vossert I met when they first moved in." He paused for dra-
matic effect. And to catch his breath. "That Mrs. Vossert
had part of a finger missing and this Mrs. Vossert doesn't,
but both Mrs. Vosserts wear the same jewelry and they
both go by the name Sidney. Actually, I should have
known something was wrong because the first Mrs. Vos-

sert wasn't around for a week or so, and then all of a sudden she reappears, only even at the time I didn't think it was the same person." Whew, Matt was having a hard time keeping up. By now Julie was practically trotting, and as she glanced at him, a scowl pulled her eyebrows into a single perplexed line.

"Matt, what are you talking about?"

All of a sudden, Tebby was between them, the stick clenched in her strong teeth. Matt pulled it out, heaved it toward the dunes, and Tebby was off again.

"Look," Matt tried to explain, "Tebby keeps digging in one certain spot over by Bluff Cottage. It's right where I saw Vossert messing around with a pick and shovel, and I think . . . maybe . . . that is, it's possible that Tebby's found . . . I don't know for sure, but things are so weird up there, I think maybe Tebby's found the place where Vossert buried his . . . buried a . . . buried his wife . . ."

Julie stopped in her tracks and stared. "Oh, come on, Matt. You've been watching too much TV. My dogs dig holes all over the place and haven't found a body yet. Besides, you said you just saw Mrs. Vossert yesterday."

Tebby was back, eagerly nudging Matt with the stick. Just to get rid of her, he took the stick and flung it as far as he could.

"You're not listening, Julie." Frantic to be understood and beyond the point of tact, Matt was practically shouting. "I just told you it's not the same Mrs. Vossert. The first Mrs. Vossert has been missing since she first arrived, though the second Mrs. Vossert is wearing her jewelry. That proves it right there."

"Proves what? I don't see that it proves anything." Julie started up again, only now she was almost running.

What was the matter with her that she didn't understand? "Don't you see, Julie, the whole set-up is phony. It's as phony as the morning I saw Vossert strangle . . ." Wait a minute. He still hadn't found the slot where that piece of the puzzle fit. The Vosserts had put on their murder act for some unknown reason he hadn't figured out yet and with no explanation to offer, he'd better forget that one for now.

But Julie had already picked up on it. "Strangle! You saw Vossert strangle someone?"

"Yes, I mean no, he didn't really strangle her, though that's what they both made it look like. They were pretending, putting on an act to . . ."

"Listen, Matt," Julie interrupted, "maybe it would be better if we talked some other time when there isn't a gale blowing and I don't have math homework to finish before school. If there's a body around, it'll still be there tomorrow unless it disappears again." Without even waiting for Matt's reply, Julie turned and headed down the beach at a good clip.

Matt watched her go. *If* there is a body. Forget it. Julie didn't understand or believe anything he had said, and if she thought he was going to talk about it with her some other time, she was mistaken. What was it with Julie and him anyway? They got along fine the other day, at least after Julie made an effort to smooth things over. Now here they were locking horns again. And today Matt had really needed to talk to someone. Well, what did Julie matter? She was just a Cape Cod icicle after all.

Matt felt a wet nose nudge him. It was Tebby with her stick again. "You're like a yo-yo, Tebby," Matt complained as he whipped the stick over the dunes. "But at least I can count on you. Not like some people I know," he added to himself. Well, if Julie wasn't going to help him, he'd have to go ahead and check into this on his own.

Nevertheless, when Matt's alarm went off at 2:30 the next morning and he lay in bed watching the little red digital numbers click by, he had no interest in going ahead with anything. But Tebby wouldn't let him be. She sat up at the foot of his bed and barked as if to get rid of him so she could go back to sleep. Matt knew he didn't have a chance. He groaned and rolled out of bed.

He wasn't surprised to find Nimicut Salt Marsh blanketed in a fog that looked solid enough to walk on. All the way over on his bike, precariously balancing a shovel on his handlebars and bemoaning the lack of a car, he had pedaled through pockets of fog as thick as smoke.

He shoved his bike under a juniper shrub, took his shovel and headed toward the two pine trees only fifty yards or so down from the Vosserts'. Bluff Cottage was dark now, with all the draperies drawn. The fog lapped at the edges of the marsh, draping the hollows, but not quite reaching up as far as the two pine trees. Dark clouds skittered across the almost full moon so that light and shadows flickered on and off, in and out, like a faulty fluorescent bulb. That was okay with Matt. The more shadows there were, the better he was hidden. Beyond him, the dense marsh fog was alive with night noises, creaks and scurryings and hoots and rustlings. One cry sounded like a wailing baby. Prickles of goose bumps ran up Matt's arms as the weeping rose and fell, echoing in the windless air.

Matt picked up his shovel, and as he did a projectile, heavy and silent, swept over his head with a rush of air. Stunned, he could only stare as the dark shape fluttered out over the marsh. And then the cloud cover parted, the moon shone white and Matt could clearly see the wide wings, the big body, the wobbly flight pattern. An owl. Wak-wak-wak, it cried mournfully.

Matt wiped his damp palms on his jeans. He had to be out of his mind digging around out here in the middle of the night by the light of the moon. A silly rhyme his father used to sing went through his head.

> The big baboon by the light of the moon
> Was combing his auburn hair.

> *The monkey he got drunk*
> *Sat on the elephant's trunk*
> *The elephant sneezed and fell on his knees*
> *And that was the end of the monk,*
> *the monk, the monk.* ·

Maybe he was a baboon, combing his hair by the light of the moon, crazy like everyone thought, imagining missing fingers and disappearing wives. No, he wasn't. He knew what he had seen and he knew that he was right. Vossert wasn't going to get away with this. Matt would show them who was watching too much TV.

He went back to his digging. It wasn't as if he were going to go down deep. He'd just dig far enough to find some kind of evidence . . .

"STOP!"

Matt didn't know whether it was the barked command behind him or the sudden blaze of lights he reacted to first. Whichever it was, he spun around, his eyes wide with fright. There was nothing to see but three blinding discs of light veined by trailing wisps of fog.

"This is Constable Hulse," came a disembodied voice from behind the glare. "Put your shovel on the ground and walk back toward me slowly."

16

Vossert, of course, was behind it. Matt found that out as soon as Constable Hulse got him to the little gray-shingled building that looked like just another summer cottage but was, in fact, the police station. Apparently, Vossert had seen Matt digging, called the police and signed a complaint against him for trespassing. As it turned out, the area between the two pine trees was on Bluff Cottage property and not in Nimicut Salt Marsh at all.

"But, Constable Hulse, trespassing has nothing to do with it." Matt ran his fingers through his hair. It was tousled and snarled from where the damp night air had curled it tight. "Vossert's wife has disappeared. She hasn't been around for weeks and that place where I was digging is important . . . it's . . . I think . . ." Matt stopped. Even now he couldn't bring himself to voice his suspicions to Constable Hulse, not after he'd accused Vossert of murder once before and had the whole thing blow up in his face. But somehow, some way, he had to make Constable Hulse understand.

They sat on opposite sides of a scarred old desk that was covered with dusty bowling trophies in a little box of a room that smelled of steam heat, stale coffee and pipe smoke. Though the walls were freshly painted battleship gray and hung with faded portraits of every president back to Hoover, the room still looked dingy. Constable Hulse lit up his pipe, tipped back in his chair and studied Matt with a mild expression on his long face. "Now you know better'n that. Mrs. Vossert is home safe in bed where you oughtta be."

"I tell you that isn't Vossert's wife. Part of Mrs. Vossert's middle finger is missing and this new woman has got all five. It's two different people. The first one disappeared and this second one is wearing her jewelry." By now Matt was leaning over the desk so far he was face to face with Constable Hulse.

"Look, your family goes back in East Tedham a good spell." Constable Hulse's tone was reasonable. "Your mother's Uncle Harry was a pal of mine. I don't hold anything against you, but you gotta lay off these Vosserts or you'll be deep in hot water. As it is, your court appearance is gonna be tough. The Juvenile Board's been clamping down real hard lately on offenders."

The radiator knocked and hissed and Matt didn't know if the room was really hot or if he was just burning up with frustration. Like Julie, Constable Hulse wasn't listening. "Will you check out that place down from Vossert's house yourself? Will you, please?" Matt urged through clenched teeth.

Constable Hulse took the pipe out of his mouth and brought his chair back to the floor with a bang. He riveted Matt with his washed-out blue eyes that were just like Mrs. Shreve's. Matt wondered irrelevantly if living on Cape Cod did that to people's eyes or whether everyone was descended from the same blue-eyed Pilgrim ancestors. "I heard you real clear, Runyon, now you hear me." Constable Hulse enunciated each word as if Matt were deaf and had to lip-read. "Sergeant Fleming investigated that area just now and nothing is buried there but old bones and garbage. Get that? No body. No wife. No nothing."

Matt heard a gasp but was so shocked he didn't realize it had come from him. "I don't believe it."

"Believe it."

"Vossert must have dug up whatever was there before your man arrived." That had to be it.

Constable Hulse stood up. "Sergeant Fleming and I answered that call at the same time. Garbage is what he found 'n garbage is what was buried. Now, before you go I wanta make one thing clear. Knock off this preoccupation with Vossert. We've answered three calls out there involving you 'n this is the end of it. Forever. You understand?"

Matt nodded without even knowing what he had agreed to. It was unbelievable that there was only garbage and bones buried between those two pine trees. It didn't even make sense. Garbage and old bones certainly would have attracted Tebby, but why would Vossert have bothered? He must have weekly garbage pick-up like everyone else in East Tedham.

Matt turned down Constable Hulse's offer of a ride home. Right now he needed time to himself and the long walk from the station house would do it. Besides, he wanted to go by way of Nimicut Salt Marsh to pick up his bike and shovel before some passerby ripped them off.

Fog still haunted the hollows of the road. Although the moon had set and there wasn't a star to be seen, there was no trace yet of dawn. Matt shivered. The night seemed even colder and damper than before as if it were taking a last stand against the coming warmth of the day. He picked up a stick and whipped it along the high grass by the side of the road. No evidence. No body. No nothing. He should have felt relieved, even good. After all, his mother had called from Denver and although there had been a postponement of the hearing, things out there looked promising. And when Matt had checked up on Mrs. Shreve, he had found out she was doing pretty well and hadn't had a heart attack like Dr. Grogan first thought. So why did he feel frustrated? Checkmated? Angry? Because he knew deep down that Mrs. Vossert #1 was still missing. Something had happened to her and no one would believe him, not Constable Hulse, not Julie.

By now he had reached the path that led into the marsh. He made his way past the familiar snaggy briars and prickly brambles to Black Rock. In the past hours, the fog had lifted enough for him to see Bluff Cottage clearly across the marsh. There were no lights on, but that didn't mean Vossert wasn't awake and watching for him. Matt sensed that Vossert was always watching for him, always aware of what he was doing.

Sudden anger flushed Matt's face as he thought of how Vossert had sucked him into his life the way the thick mud of the marsh at low tide sucked at his feet. And Vossert's life was just as dark and mysterious as the marsh mud. Here Matt was, booked for a court appearance and all because of Vossert. Booked. For the first time Matt registered on what that meant. He was considered a criminal. At the realization, a terrible fury roiled up inside him, overwhelming him like the waves of the ocean that crashed on the beach, then pulled back before mounting again. The physical intensity of his anger was so staggering he had to lean against Black Rock and close his eyes to steady himself. He stood braced on the rock for long minutes, fighting for control over the pounding inside him.

When he opened his eyes, something to the east glinted crimson. It was the sliver of the red sun breaking into a streaky pink sky. As Matt watched it come up over the horizon, he couldn't ever remember seeing a sun quite like it, as burning red and angry as he himself felt. Now its rays stretched toward the marsh, lighting up the brown grasses. Only Matt realized the sere browns were freshening with new spring-green shoots. And the waking marsh was alive with sound—the scratching of an animal somewhere, peeps, croaks, hooting. A pair of black ducks cruised down and landed with silent ripples on the flat surface of one of the narrow tidal creeks.

Gradually the pressure eased as Matt's neck and shoulders loosened and he breathed more evenly. How long he stood leaning against Black Rock, he didn't know, but when he first saw the fox, the sun was well over the horizon and only cobwebs of fog still laced the marsh.

It was the same red fox Matt had seen before, more gray than red. He was crouched low, with his ears alert and his dark eyes riveted on something ahead of him. It was a good-sized bird with black and white bands limping toward one of the creek banks. Its right wing dragged on the ground as it flopped helplessly along. The fox crept closer.

It never occurred to Matt to interfere. He was a helpless bystander at an impending disaster. Pounce! The fox bounded high in the air and came down with all four paws together. But the moment the fox made his move, the bird took off into the air with a strong beat of both wings. As it mounted higher and higher, the fox raised his narrow head to follow its flight before he stole off into the grass himself. He must have felt as dumbfounded as Matt. There wasn't anything wrong with the bird's wing at all. That fluttering and limping had been an act. The bird probably had a nest nearby and was luring the fox away from it by pretending to be an easy prey. Ironically, it was the same trick that the fox had played on Tebby when he had lured her away from his den by acting as bait himself.

This innocent looking little salt marsh wasn't so innocent after all. It was a slice of harsh reality. Everything in it was surviving on its own terms, just like the world outside. The world outside. The realization hit Matt with the force of a physical blow. Vossert had been playing the very same game. He had been luring the police away from his den all this time, too, only he had used Matt for bait.

It was suddenly so obvious, Matt didn't understand why he hadn't figured it out before. When Vossert had seen Matt staring at his wife in Dr. Grogan's office, he recognized Matt as a serious threat. After all, Matt had seen and talked to the first Mrs. Vossert, maybe even noticed her missing finger. Vossert knew he had to do something about Matt. But what? His line of thinking was easy enough to follow.

Matt had already sent in one false alarm to the police on the morning the Vosserts had arrived. Vossert realized that if he could con Matt into calling in another false alarm, the police would never pay attention to Matt again. About anything. Knowing what time Matt walked Tebby, and knowing that Matt watched Bluff Cottage through binoculars, Vossert had arranged his act. He had opened his draperies and then he and his wife had staged her murder. And Matt had fallen for it hook, line and sinker. Vossert had counted on Matt calling the police and that was just what he had done.

Now Vossert was ready for his next move. He had already set up the scenario in case he needed it by making sure Matt saw him digging between those two pitch pines. Next he buried old bones and garbage there to attract Tebby. It was as if he could read Matt's mind. Sure that Matt would become suspicious and take action, Vossert had lain in wait for Matt to show up and start digging. Then he'd called the police and signed a complaint. Vossert knew that little episode would wipe out any residue of credibility Matt might have had with the police. And it had.

Lured . . . manipulated . . . tricked. Matt had been all those. But no more. He was on to Vossert now and police or no police, somehow, some way, he would find evidence against Vossert that would prove he was right.

17

As soon as Matt got home from Nimicut Salt Marsh, he let Tebby out, took a shower, ate a mammoth breakfast and went to bed. School wasn't a consideration. He felt like he'd been up forever instead of just since 2:30. Besides, it was Friday and with spring vacation starting next week, the teachers had long since finished with anything that mattered.

A few hours later, when Matt woke up, he knew what he had to do. He had to get inside Bluff Cottage. It was a risk. Even dangerous. But he had to find some kind of evidence to pin on Vossert. The problem was how to get in. Unfortunately, the Vosserts had canceled their account with Pettingill's so he couldn't use the excuse of delivering groceries. Maybe he could phone that there had been an accident and to come immediately to the hospital. No good. Matt couldn't think of one single person the Vosserts would rush to the hospital for.

It wasn't until that afternoon that a solution came to him. When he delivered groceries to a house with a FOR SALE sign out front, he remembered that Mrs. Shreve had said that Bluff Cottage had been on the market for a year.

When Matt's house in Colorado had been up for sale, realtors liked to show it when the family was out. That maneuver might work with Bluff Cottage. Matt could call, say he was a realtor and wanted to show Bluff Cottage some time when the Vosserts were out.

The hitch was the Vosserts were sure to recognize Matt's voice, even on the phone. Mrs. Shreve would probably be game enough to call for him, but she was still in the hospital. Mr. Pettingill? Forget it. That was it, Matt's total list of candidates. Except for one. Julie. In the back of his mind, Matt had known all along that it would boil down to Julie, though Julie was a problem too. Their last meeting hadn't ended on exactly cordial terms. In fact, Julie hadn't believed one word he'd said. To be fair, he'd been pretty whipped up himself. But not today. Today he'd have it all together and be as laid back as Constable Hulse.

Matt woke up Saturday morning even before the alarm went off. "D Day, Tebs," he called. "We're about to hit the beaches."

He didn't even bother to glance at Bluff Cottage as he slipped his bike under a bayberry bush and trotted along the path with Tebby around the soggy edges of the marsh to the sluice bridge. As he crossed the narrow wooden bridge, he noticed how high the water was as it spilled over the sluice. There were only a couple of inches between the water and the underside of the bridge before the water cascaded into the marsh in a raging torrent. The full moon, combined with high spring tides, had drastically raised the water level. Much higher and it would be over the bridge itself.

It was a sullen kind of morning on the beach, with grim clouds scudding over a steel-gray sea. Luckily, Matt didn't have long to wait. There Julie was, jogging along in the hard-packed sand by the water's edge. Matt jumped up and ran down to meet her. She smiled when she saw him and waved. It was an auspicious beginning.

Matt smiled in return and fell in with her pace. "Hi, Julie."

"Hi, Matt." This time her smile was broader. "When you weren't in school yesterday, I hoped you weren't sick again."

Even better. She sounded concerned. "No, I had some things to take care of."

"Oh."

They ran in unison for a few minutes without talking. Tebby ran along with them, splashing in and out of the water and spraying them every time she shook herself. On Saturday, Matt wasn't due at Pettingill's until 11:00, which gave him plenty of time to make his move.

"You said before we should talk when we weren't in a hurry. So how's now?" He tried to sound casual.

Julie pushed up her sleeve to check her watch. "That's okay, I guess. Dad's picking me up at noon to spend the weekend with him in Boston."

Good. Julie was in no hurry either. Matt didn't say anything more as they continued to trot along at a steady pace. He was even able to keep up without getting too winded, which was a triumph in itself. Granted, the wind was at their backs, but he felt good, and for the moment, the running, the sound of the crashing surf and the raucous chatter of the gulls was enough.

"Well?" Julie finally asked.

"Well what?"

"Well, you said you wanted to talk. So I'm listening."

Matt paused for effect. "I got arrested Thursday night. That's why I wasn't in school."

Julie, slowing down, glanced at Matt but didn't stop. "What for?"

"Trespassing on Vossert's property."

Now she did stop. "I don't believe it. Why would you do that?"

Matt stopped too so that the two of them faced each other. Julie's eyes were gray today. They seemed to change as the color of the ocean changed, from blue to green to gray. "I was so sure that something had happened to Mrs. Vossert that I went digging in the middle of the night to find evidence. I didn't know it, but I was on Vossert's property. Vossert saw me, called the police and had me arrested." There, he had been concise, rational and even laid back.

Julie pursed her lips in exasperation. "Did you find anything?"

Matt cleared his throat, feeling a little less laid back. "Well, no, but that doesn't mean something weird isn't going on."

Without discussing it, they had both turned and headed toward the dunes. A long piece of driftwood was just wide enough for the two of them to sit on. "You see," Matt started to explain, "Vossert has manipulated me from the day . . ."

"Matt, what is it with you and these Vosserts anyway? It's like you're obsessed with them," Julie interrupted. As she spoke, she took out a pack of gum, unwrapped a piece and folded it in her mouth.

Matt turned a furious face toward her. "I don't know why you can't keep quiet for two minutes and let me talk. Every time I try to tell you something you jump in and interrupt. And do you have to chew that everlasting gum like some kind of cow chewing its cud?" Matt's heart was pumping harder than it had the whole time he had been jogging.

Julie's expression closed right down and her eyebrows pulled together in that familiar tight line. She pushed herself up off the driftwood. "Matt, we don't seem to do a very good job of communicating."

Matt grabbed her arm. "Wait. I have a plan and . . ."

Julie shook her head. "No, I don't want any part of a plan that involves the Vosserts. Really, Matt, I'd like to go. I didn't jog at all yesterday and I won't have a chance to jog for the rest of the weekend." She pulled her arm away and before Matt could say anything more, headed down the beach at a good clip.

Here we go again, Matt thought. Every time he and Julie got together, they clashed. Now he was back in limbo, with no plan, and worse, no Julie. He picked up a piece of old snow-fencing and angrily heaved it as far as he could into the water. There was an immediate flash of black from behind him as Tebby plunged into the booming surf after it.

Tebby was lucky. Everything was a game to Tebby. Distracted by his thoughts, Matt only half watched as Tebby breasted the first wave succcessfully. But before she could steady her course, a second wave came along and dashed her under. There, her head was up again as she paddled easily over the next wave. Now Matt was watching intently as another wave, close behind the first, flung her over almost backwards. Still she didn't give up. She headed straight into a giant breaker that was just cresting. Predictably, that one slammed her down too.

Matt remembered what Mrs. Shreve had said about swimming in the surf. The more you fight the waves, the faster the ocean defeats you. It was true. Tebby could see the stick floating in the water ahead of her, but every time she got anywhere near it, a wave clobbered her. Tebby should have been working with the waves, swimming to her goal from an angle, like Mrs. Shreve had said. She'd never reach the stick the way she was going at it now.

And she didn't. The next time Tebby surfaced, she was swimming toward the beach. She had given up. But as she paddled for shore, one wave after another hurtled her toward land, then sucked her back into the surf with the undertow. She had only a short distance to swim, but it took her forever to make it. When she finally staggered up on the beach, her tongue was lolling and her sides heaved with exhaustion.

"Oh, Tebby, you'll never learn, will you?" Matt stroked her quivering body. "You have to fight every wave just like me."

Just like me. Matt paused as Tebby looked at him with red-rimmed eyes. Just like me, he repeated. Maybe Mrs. Shreve hadn't been talking only about swimming that day. Maybe she had been talking about him. Maybe she was saying that Matt was defeating himself by battling every wave that came along instead of letting the current do the work. His temper. That was what she had been talking about. She was telling Matt that his temper was defeating him like fighting the waves had defeated Tebby.

His temper had certainly defeated him just now with Julie. Not that Julie wasn't quick on the trigger too. Still, he had blown first, then she'd jumped in. And that gum. She knew her gum drove him crazy. But why do you let it? Matt could almost hear Mrs. Shreve ask. Just raise your annoyance level. You're pounding away at the surf like Tebby, letting every little thing beat you down. Your anger is controlling you instead of you controlling your anger.

But he couldn't help it. His mother had a temper and Matt was just like her. Look how she and Warren used to fight and bicker all the time. But was fighting and bickering what Matt wanted? No, it wasn't, and Julie didn't want it either. That day he had delivered groceries to her house, she had been the one to make up.

Matt leaned down and rubbed Tebby's bedraggled coat. Though she was still panting and wheezing, her whole body was tensely alert. Something down the beach was attracting her attention. The piece of snow-fencing Matt had thrown in the water had washed up on the sand. But Tebby was too exhausted to fetch it.

"You did yourself in on that one, Tebby." Matt gave a short laugh. "Fighting the waves head-on doesn't seem to work any better for you than it does for me. I think it's about time we tried something different."

18

Swimming with the current turned out to be a whole lot harder than Matt had anticipated. He stopped Julie on her way back up the beach, but she gave him a big song-and-dance about why she didn't have time to talk.

He took the plunge. "I . . . I'm sorry I blew up before, Julie. It's just that I'm uptight about getting arrested, you know? But I'm okay now, I promise. And I won't blow again." He tried to smile to show her that he meant it, but that took effort too.

"I don't know, Matt. We've hashed it over before and never seem to get anywhere. Why go through it again?"

"Because . . . because . . ." The words were hard to get out. ". . . because I need help, Julie, and you're the only one I can turn to."

Julie's closed expression suddenly softened and now her eyes looked more blue than gray. "Since you put it that way, how can I refuse?"

So the two of them went back to their piece of driftwood, sat down and talked. And as they talked, Julie drew patterns in the sand, curlicues and swirls and wriggles, while Matt filled his hands with the coarse grains and let them sift through his fingers like an upended hourglass. Tebby, who had been behind the dunes chasing a rabbit, finally gave up and settled at their feet and dozed. The tide rolled in high, even higher than the strip of seaweed and shells and trash that marked the previous high water line. The sky darkened and the sun disappeared completely behind a thick cloud cover.

Still they talked. Matt had to do a lot of arguing to convince Julie that somehow something had happened to the first Mrs. Vossert. And it took a whole lot more arguing to make her understand that he had to get into Bluff Cottage to look around. At one juncture, they even started their usual shouting match. But Matt choked back that old familiar hard lump of anger and they resolved it without stalking off in opposite directions.

"What happens if you get caught breaking into the house? With your record, you could end up at Wyckoff Juvenile Detention Center." Julie made a box in the sand with bars across it like the window of a jail.

"I won't get caught. I won't even go near the house until I'm sure the Vosserts are gone."

Julie looked thoughtful when Matt told her about his real estate plan. "My Aunt Elizabeth works for Dobbins Realty in town. I guess I could pretend I was Aunt Elizabeth calling from Dobbins."

It was perfect. Julie even had a throaty kind of voice that made her sound older than she was.

"You can ask the Vosserts when they'll be out so you can show their house when it's empty," Matt elaborated. "And maybe you could get some business cards from your aunt. Any time a realtor took someone through our house, they left a business card on the hall table."

"Yeah, I guess I could pick up a couple." Julie still looked pensive as she studied the jail design she'd drawn in

111

the sand. Then, decisively, she wiped it out. "Okay, Matt, I'll do it." At his instantly enthusiastic expression, she held up her hand. "On two conditions, one, that you come to our next Muir Club meeting when we discuss the ORV trail and two, that you come to the special town forum Thursday night on ORV restrictions."

The off-road vehicle trail. Julie just wouldn't give up. Here he was talking life and death and she was talking environment. Matt opened his mouth to say no, he wouldn't go, that the ORV trail was okay, that as far as he was concerned, it was harmless and fun. But he didn't. The price of refusing put him right back to Square One. He swallowed his retort and stuck out his hand. "It's a deal."

Julie grinned as she shook it. "Deal."

Matt was surprised at the feel of her hand. Julie was tall and somehow he had always thought of her as big, but her hand was so narrow and small-boned, it completely disappeared in his. Her feet were small and narrow too, he realized. So was her face, although high cheekbones and wide-spaced eyes disguised its slightness. And for the first time, Matt noticed that Julie's eyelashes curled back almost double. He'd never seen eyelashes like that and he wondered if they were fake. Of course they weren't. Julie didn't even use makeup so why would she wear false eyelashes? It was a moment before Matt was aware that Julie was blushing under his inspection. To break the intimacy, she jumped up and brushed the sand off her sweat pants.

"I'll race you back," she challenged.

At this particular moment, Matt could have licked the world. "You're on."

A startled Tebby leapt up too and joined Julie in her charge down the beach. Matt let them get a fair distance ahead, then started after them. It was maddening. As hard as he ran, he couldn't catch up. What started out on his part as a casual sort of race suddenly became a full-blown contest. Julie turned around once to size up their positions and when she saw how far back he was, she laughed. When the wind threaded her laughter back to him, he put out all the way. But now that his first burst of adrenaline was used up, he was getting winded and falling farther and farther behind. This stupid mono still handicapped him whether he was over it or not. He headed for the water's edge where the sand was hard and compact, and although that helped some, he still couldn't catch up.

Closer and closer. There, at last he overtook her. Or maybe she allowed him to overtake her. Either way, Matt was so exhausted that when he reached her, he grabbed her in a gesture of only half-hidden anger and pulled her down on the sand. But when she saw his expression, she rolled out of his reach, jumped up and ran toward the dunes, laughing the whole way.

Exhausted or not, he was right behind her and this time when he overtook her, he seized her around the waist and pulled her down on her back. The sand flew as Julie twisted and struggled to get away. But Matt had a firm grip. In seconds, he had her hands pinned down and he was kneeling over her. She was still laughing. Laughing at Matt. He was gasping for breath and raging inside. And then a cold spray showered over him. It was Tebby, shaking herself after a swim. It was like a rain storm dousing a fire. Unexpected laughter welled up inside him and suddenly he and Julie were laughing together.

Then they were looking hard at each other and neither of them was laughing. Julie's hair was full of sand. A couple of grains were even sprinkled in her eyebrows. Matt reached down and carefully brushed them out. As he did, Julie raised her head and Matt leaned forward and kissed her. Her lips were wet and salty and parted just a little. And then she was kissing him back. He pulled her up to a sitting position and put his arms around her. Her arms

113

were around him too, and he could feel her strong, fast heartbeat. He didn't know if her heartbeat was fast because of their race or because of him. He tasted the faint flavor of salt and in his mind the ocean and the running and perspiration were all mixed up.

Julie drew back a little and studied Matt's face as if taking stock. She must have been satisfied with what she saw, because she closed her eyes and they kissed again. And as they kissed Matt felt his own pulse rate go faster and faster. After a moment, Julie pulled away. She raised her hand and traced first around his right ear and then around his left.

"Hey, Matt, I like your crazy ears."

Matt ran his finger over the little bump in her nose. "And I like your crazy nose."

Neither of them said anything more. Then Julie shook her head hard a couple of times and brushed her fingers through her hair to get out the sand. "Dad will be waiting for me and I'm freezing. I'd better go."

Matt nodded without arguing. Arguing would have spoiled it. They were both grinning like two kids at a circus as Julie gave Matt a quick kiss that landed somewhere on his chin, then rubbed Tebby's head before starting off. Matt watched her run the whole length of the beach until she was out of sight around a curve in the shoreline. She set an effortless, easy kind of pace, and even in her baggy sweat suit, had a trim, lean look. Spare was a better word. Spare in form, spare in manner. Even spare in sharing herself.

Back in Colorado, Matt had always liked small, giggly cheerleader types who knew how to flirt and carry on a conversation so that he never had to extend himself. Certainly none of them were no-nonsense girls like Julie, who knew her own mind and took a stand for what she believed in. All of a sudden, Matt realized a giggly cheerleader type wasn't so appealing any more. Julie had changed all that. It was hard to believe what had happened. Matt Runyon interested in a Cape Cod codfish? Not very likely. But there it was, a fact.

19

That afternoon it started raining even before Matt finished making his Pettingill deliveries. By the time he stopped to see Mrs. Shreve at the hospital and headed for home, the northeast wind was whipping such sheets of rain at him, he had to get off his bike and walk it up Old Duckhole Road.

Despite the rain, Matt was glad he had stopped at the hospital. Mrs. Shreve had been pleased to see him, and even if she didn't look terrific, at least her eyes weren't that lifeless, milky blue any more. Matt had made up his mind to tell her about his plan for getting into Bluff Cottage, but her daughter Donna was there, a forty-year-old taller, heavier version of what Mrs. Shreve must have once looked like, and the three of them never got beyond discussing trivialities like the weather.

Only the weather wasn't so trivial. By the time Matt wheeled his bike into the garage, his hair was already plastered down flat. Cold rivulets of water trickled down his neck and he was shivering. It didn't seem possible that this nor'easter, as Mrs. Shreve called it, could last for three days the way she predicted. If that were so, all of East Tedham would end up underwater.

Matt tried to open the back door, but the damp wood was swollen and he couldn't budge it. Unfortunately, Tebby had heard him and was frantic on the other side to get out. She had been in all day and she could last only so long. There, by slamming his shoulder hard against the door, Matt was able to open it. Tebby bolted past him, squatted in the grass by the back door and then raced back into the house. Matt had to laugh. Even a retriever wasn't about to stay outside in this wild weather.

Matt stripped off his wet jacket and threw it over the radiator. As he dried his hair with a dish towel, he mentally flushed Cape Cod down the drain. Damp, damper, dampest. Wet, wetter, wettest. Cape Cod, Caper Codder, Capest Coddest. Yuck. A hot shower coming up. Matt had already started up the stairs when he heard an abrasive scraping sound above the wail of the wind.

Scritch-scratch. Scritch-scratch.

He froze, one foot half raised between steps.

Scritch-scratch. Scritch-scratch.

Someone was tapping to get in. Matt's ears seemed almost to expand as he strained to pinpoint where the grating noise was coming from. Upstairs. It had come from upstairs. Someone was trying to get in an upstairs window. Vossert. As Matt stood there paralyzed breathing in short panicked gasps, Tebby pushed past him and loped up the rest of the stairs. She stood at the top looking quizzically down with a "Well, what's with you?" kind of expression.

Her unconcern released Matt. If anyone was trying to break in, for sure Tebby would have reacted. Scritch-scratch. Scritch-scratch. The tapping was regular and unvarying. It wasn't Vossert trying to get in. It was something hitting against the house, like a shutter. Matt expired all the air in his lungs with one long, relieved, chest-deflating sigh.

The noise seemed to be coming from his mother's bedroom. Sure enough, when Matt went in, he saw that a branch from an ancient apple tree outside her window had broken off and was tapping against the house. Matt opened the window and snapped off the branch. But instead of heading for the shower, he lingered. His mother's room smelled faintly of the cologne she always used and her desk by the window was the usual jumble of books, articles, clippings and carbons, with notes Scotch-taped all over the lampshade.

All of a sudden, Matt missed his mother terribly. The custody proceedings out in Denver had been postponed again, though when Matt had talked to her, she felt optimistic. Still, she didn't think she and Bucky would be back until the end of next week. It wasn't just that Matt was tired of hamburgers and pizzas and the frozen stuff he bought at Pettingill's which he never seemed to thaw long enough, but he hated not having another presence in the house besides Tebby. Even if Mom was still at work when he got home, her presence was always there, filling up the empty spaces. Now there was no presence at all.

Not even Bucky's. With the realization that Bucky might be leaving to live with Warren, Matt had suddenly seen Bucky as more than just a pest of a kid brother who always wanted to watch cartoons on TV or who nagged him day and night to play ball. In this past week, Bucky had become a real presence of his own, and Matt missed him, too.

He closed his mother's door quietly behind him and stripped for his shower. But as he took off his shirt and jeans, he still felt edgy and tense and that surprised him. He had never minded staying alone in the house before, but now he was aware of every creak and groan of the old floorboards and mismatched joints from where the house had been hastily slapped together as a summer cottage The steam radiators knocked and banged. The rain drummed against the windows in an uneven tattoo and the wind snuffled and snored and wheezed as if in the throes of a monstrous asthma attack.

But worse than the noise was that once the shower was on, Matt couldn't hear anything. Not the back door opening where he hadn't been able to fix the lock, nor footsteps on the stairs, nor a heavy tread across the uncarpeted upstairs hall. Nothing. He was trapped and helpless behind the shower curtain. Vos-sert. Vos-sert. The massage unit attached to the shower head slammed the name into Matt's body with every pulsing beat. Vos-sert. Vos-sert. Usually Matt took his time in the shower, but not tonight. Tonight he was in and out fast.

As the evening wore on, it didn't seem possible that the storm could get any worse, but it did. The rain drove across the empty lot next door with such force, Matt couldn't even see the old cedar tree at the end of the front walk. Water gushed and gurgled from the downspouts. For the first time ever, water leaked in around the windows in the living room. Matt mopped it up, then stuffed rags around the sills. Every drawer, window and door was distended and jammed. The whole house seemed to be as swollen and aching as he had been when he had mono. At nine o'clock, he decided to go to bed just to get the day over with.

Tebby woke him up. She salt bolt upright at the foot of his bed with a growl rumbling deep in her chest. Matt was instantly awake. He glanced at the clock. Blood-red numbers shone in a raven-black night. 3:14. Something was wrong. Matt sensed it in his gut. The rain and the wind still howled and tore into the house, but that wasn't it. What was wrong was not a noise, but a lack of noise. Matt lay still a moment with his heart beating such a drumfire, the covers rose and fell with it. Suddenly he realized what it was. The sump pump in the basement wasn't working. It usually provided a background drone that was so constant he didn't even notice it. But now that the humming was stilled, its silence shrieked for attention. He'd have to check it out. If he didn't the whole basement could flood.

Tebby followed so close on his heels, Matt almost tripped over her. Knowing that the basement was lit by only a single electric bulb, Matt grabbed a flashlight as he passed through the kitchen. Actually, it wasn't an authentic basement. It was just a narrow little root cellar with a poured concrete floor that had once been dirt. Half the area was taken up by an enormous coal bin that was now used for storage but which Bucky claimed was where the Cellar Monsters lived. Cellar Monsters. Ridiculous. Bucky, who could even describe them, swore that he'd come upon them once by surprise. He insisted they slept in the coal bin by day and haunted by night. Hyperactive imagination was what haunted Bucky. Nevertheless, as Matt started down the basement stairs, he reached for Tebby just to reassure himself she was still there.

It was the sump pump all right. As soon as Matt shone his flashlight on the basement floor he saw big puddles where the ground water had seeped up through the concrete. Careful not to stand in any water, he reached up and pulled the cord on the electric bulb. It swung back and forth, throwing light, dark, light, dark across the low-ceilinged little room. On one swing, Matt caught a glimpse of the high half-window over by the furnace where the coal used to be delivered down the chute and into the bin. The window was open and the rain was pouring in. Matt stared in disbelief as a gust of damp air chilled him. The window was open and he hadn't opened it.

His mother. Maybe his mother had opened it. Or the wind . . . or . . . it didn't matter. He'd have to close it. But that meant maneuvering behind the dark coal bin where there was no light at all. On second thought, he'd close it tomor . . .

"SSSssss. Mi-aullllll." A strident scream with no definable dimensions shrilled through the basement. It was a cry of such torment and agony it didn't seem to have a beginning or an end. It just filled all the space, reverberating in Matt's head like a clanging cymbal.

Simultaneously, a violent scrambling and clattering erupted in the coal bin as a long, black terrorized form shot out and up the stairs. With his flashlight still idiotically focused on the open window, Matt dimly reacted. Tebby, that was Tebby charging out of the coal bin and up the stairs. But that hadn't been Tebby's tortured caterwauling. What or who it had been Matt couldn't even imagine. In one swift motion, he spun around to run upstairs himself. But his foot landed in a puddle and his legs shot out from under him. He barely caught himself in time as he flailed his arms to keep his balance. Lurching and stumbling he made it up the stairs three at a time to the top, then slammed the door shut behind him. But the frame was swollen and the door wouldn't close all the way. Cursing and swearing, he put his shoulder to it and rammed it shut. Then he shot the bolt across it. Tebby had long since disappeared, where Matt didn't know or care.

For sure Tebby had seen something in the coal bin. Bucky's Cellar Monsters. Of course it wasn't Bucky's Cellar Monsters. But that window had been open and something was down there. Vossert. It was Vossert. He had opened the window, climbed in, turned off the sump pump, then lain in wait. Knowing that Matt was onto him. Knowing that Matt planned to trap him. Knowing Matt's every move. Matt's every thought.

If only Matt had a gun, a Ruger 77. Even a handgun. But he didn't. He'd have to manage without one. Grabbing a kitchen chair, he pushed it up against the cellar door, but he rammed it so hard under the door knob, he broke off one of its legs. If only he could get away. But there was nowhere to go without a car. Besides, it didn't matter. Vossert would know where to find him.

"Meeuuw. Meeuuw."

How long the insistent cry had been coming from the other side of the basement door, Matt had no idea. But when the sound finally penetrated through his layers of fear, he realized it sounded vaguely familiar.

"Meeuuw."

A cat. It was a cat in there. It must have been a cat's scream he had heard and a cat that had frightened Tebby. Incredible. Impossible. And yet there it was, a cat. The wind must have blown the basement window open and the cat had climbed in to take shelter from the storm.

Matt's hands were trembling as he pulled back the chair, unslid the bolt and cautiously opened the basement door. A bedraggled cat blinked up at him with bright yellow eyes. It was Bingo, their neighbor's big tiger cat. She padded over to Matt and rubbed her scraggly wet fur against his legs. He went so weak with relief, he had to sit down on the top step and lean his head against the door for support.

20

"*I* don't believe it. Tell me you're kidding." Julie's tone was incredulous.

Matt didn't feel anger or resentment or regret. He didn't feel anything at all. He just shook his head without looking at Julie and continued to stare down at the ocean surging beneath the cliff. "No, I'm not kidding. I'm not going through with it."

"But what about your plans? What about me? I've phoned the Vosserts, gotten those business cards from Aunt Elizabeth's office, and now you're telling me it was all just a waste of time?" Her voice had a distinct edge of anger.

But Matt wouldn't let himself be diverted. "I'm sorry, Julie, but I've changed my mind."

"You can't. Vossert said he and his wife were going to Boston tomorrow for the day. It will be your only chance to get in their house."

"No." The matter was closed.

It was late Monday afternoon and Matt and Julie stood at the edge of her property by the cliff. Although the wind was still blowing, it had subsided considerably, and the rain had tapered off to a mist. A three-day nor'easter of middlin' force was what Mrs. Shreve had predicted and a three-day nor'easter was what they had gotten, though Matt certainly wouldn't have qualified its force as "middlin'."

It had been quite a weekend all around. First thing Sunday morning, Matt had taken the tiger cat back to its owner down the street. Then, as it continued to pour and the basement continued to flood, he had tried to fix the sump pump. About eleven o'clock, the electricity had gone off so it didn't matter whether the pump worked or not. In desperation, he had called the Fire Department to come pump out the basement, but was told there were twelve basements ahead of his. By the time the Fire Department finally arrived that afternoon, the electricity was back on and, luckily, one of the firemen was able to repair the pump. After Matt had pumped all the water out of the basement, he had spent the rest of the day cleaning up the mess.

When he had finally gotten to bed, he was beat. It wasn't even so much exhaustion as it was a kind of confusion and shock. Vossert had defeated him. Vossert had never set foot in his house, nor, as far as Matt knew, ever even tried to. It didn't matter. Vossert had violated his person, the inner being that was Matthew Runyon. Vossert had terrorized him into panicking just with the possibility of his presence. Matt was afraid of Vossert, afraid of Vossert's control over him, afraid of what Vossert would do to him, afraid . . . afraid . . . afraid . . .

The strange part was that Julie, who had been opposed to the plan to begin with, now was anxious to see it through. Monday morning she had left a message for Matt at Pettingill's that she wanted to see him. He had a delivery out her way that afternoon, so he had stopped at "Beach Plum" afterward. Julie must have been watching for him. As soon as he pulled in her driveway, she had run out in her foul-weather gear to announce that she had already phoned Vossert and picked up some business cards at her aunt's real estate office. Matt should have been elated. Instead he didn't care.

Now Julie sighed and pulled the hood of her slicker up over her head. "I certainly can't force you to do it, Matt. Actually, maybe it's just as well. If you got caught you'd be in a terrible mess. And I had such a rotten weekend with Dad and his new wife in Boston, I don't need any more hassle." Julie tried to smile but her disappointment showed through.

Matt didn't respond. He just leaned on the fence and gazed down at the ocean sixty feet below. In all his life, he had never seen anything like that surf. What a photograph it would make. The waves were moving mountains of water, storming into the land as if set on wiping out the whole shoreline. And they almost had. The battered beach was a lot narrower, with the high-water mark somewhere up past the flattened dunes and all evidence of the ORV trail wiped out. Debris had been flung everywhere, driftwood, snow-fencing, twisted pieces of metal, sections of railing, a hatch cover, smashed boat fixtures, ripped fishing nets, even broken fragments of concrete.

Matt pointed to the beach south of the cliff. "Didn't you used to have a boathouse down there by the water, Julie?" He remembered it from the day he had driven the pickup down the ORV trail.

Julie gave a splintery laugh. "High tide took the whole thing out including our two boats. The builder warned my stepfather not to build there, but he wouldn't listen. So there it is, $60,000 swept out to sea."

It wasn't even the loss of so much money that shocked Matt. It was the fact that there wasn't one single clapboard left to show that anything had been standing there at all. Demolished. Obliterated. It was the same way Vossert had canceled him out. He had no more chance of surviving against Vossert than the boathouse had been able to survive the raging sea.

But when Mrs. Shreve had been talking about survival in the ocean, she had said panic and fear can defeat a person too. Certainly panic and fear were what had been controlling Matt all weekend. And what were controlling him now. When Matt had thought Vossert was in his house, it wasn't Vossert who had wiped him out the way he'd been telling himself. His own fear had wiped him out. He had *allowed* Vossert to wipe him out. Mrs. Shreve had a point. He was no more able to deal with Vossert in the state of mind he was in now than he would be able to swim out of that surf down there. But he didn't have to let fear control him forever.

". . . probably start about 9:30. I'll pick you up if you want."

Matt wasn't aware that Julie had been talking. He looked at her blankly. "What?"

"Matt, you're not listening. I said I'd pick you up Friday night if you want to go to Jeff Tracy's party with me."

A party, Julie was asking him to a party. Any other time he would have leapt at the chance, but he had more than parties on his mind.

"Good, that sounds fine."

"Don't jump off the cliff with enthusiasm," Julie retorted.

"I am enthusiastic. It's just that I've been thinking, Julie, and . . ." Matt impulsively put his arm around her shoulders and gave her a hug. ". . . and I've decided to try and get in Bluff Cottage after all." He was grinning from ear to ear and his face was flushed with the triumph of his decision.

21

Matt was so jumpy he hardly slept Monday night. When Julie picked him up in her Land Rover at nine o'clock, he had already walked Tebby, finished cleaning the basement and finally fixed the back door lock. With Julie behind the wheel, they headed down what had once been the ORV trail, approaching the Vossert house from the north. They parked out of sight where they could keep an eye on Bluff Cottage through binoculars.

"There they go, both of them," Julie announced, half standing up. "They're pulling out of their driveway."

"Let me see." Matt reached for the binoculars but Julie wouldn't give them up.

"They're headed down the hill," she said. "Okay, they're out of sight. Let's go." With nothing more to see, Julie handed the binoculars back to Matt.

He jammed them in their case. "We're not going anywhere. You're waiting here for me the way we planned." Sometimes Julie came on just too strong. They had already decided she would wait in the Land Rover while Matt searched the house.

Not in the mood to argue, he hopped out and ran

through the low scrubby brush to the house. Vossert had said he would leave the back door key for the realtor under the mat, and sure enough, there it was. Matt let himself in and hurried through the kitchen into the living room. The place smelled so overpoweringly of cigarettes, Matt had the eerie feeling that the Vosserts were still in the house. It's just the ashtrays, he reassured himself. They were full to overflowing with butts.

As Matt looked around the living room, he felt as if he were in the middle of a stage setting that he'd previously seen from the audience. Inside, it looked different, smaller, messier, more Sears-Roebucky, as his mother would say, with a big two-story-high living room, one bedroom and bath, a kitchen, and a loft off the living room. For once, Matt was glad all the draperies were drawn. No matter how false a sense of security it gave him, being all closed in shored up his courage. He spotted a desk over by the sliding glass doors. Good. He'd start there.

Forcing himself to take his time and be methodical, he began with the Vosserts' checkbook. As far as he could tell, there was nothing out of the ordinary in it, just the usual stubs for utilities, department stores, insurance, dentist . . .

Tap, tap, tap.

Instinctively, Matt dropped to his knees. Someone was tapping on the sliding door. And this time he knew there were no trees or dead branches out there on the deck. Matt's insides congealed, his blood, his juices, even his thought processes. He just crouched there by the desk, unable to move, run, yell or even faint. Then he heard it. His name. "Matt. Matt."

Julie, it was Julie's voice calling him. Julie! As if everything were still coagulated, he made his way woodenly toward the sliding door, pulled aside the drapery and looked out on Julie's long blue-jeaned legs and beat-up run-

128

ning shoes. He let the curtain drop. Was she trying to give him a heart attack?

Bracing himself on the desk, he stood up and pulled the drapery back the whole way. There she was on the other side of the glass door, grinning in at him. Grinning. It was lucky the door was between them or he might have killed her.

Cupping her mouth, Julie called out, "I'm standing guard just in case."

Without even the strength to answer, Matt just shook his head and let the drapery drop back in place. Talk about stubborn. Julie had said she wanted to be in on this and here she was. But he didn't have time to worry about Julie. Not only was he due at Pettingill's at 11:00, but more to the point, he wanted to be in and out of here fast.

Matt rubbed his hands together to restore the circulation and went back to the checkbook. But the checkbook turned out to be a dead end. Maybe Vossert's mail would be more productive. There wasn't much, but what there was seemed to be all business correspondence from Hanna Industries, some company in Phoenix, stock reports, financial statements, legal advice, none of which meant anything to Matt.

The usual pens, pencils, paper clips, stamps and writing paper filled the drawers. A box of yellow stationery was engraved *Sidney Hanna Vossert*. Sidney Vossert was Mrs. Vossert, all right, and the Hanna part must be her middle name, or maybe her maiden name. At any rate, it was the same name as the company letterhead on Vossert's mail, Hanna Industries. Somehow Matt felt the information should have been helpful, but he had no idea what it meant. He replaced the stationery in the drawer.

Okay, now for the bedroom. Maybe he'd have better luck with the Vosserts' personal belongings. On his way down the hall, he remembered to leave one of the Dobbins

Realty cards on the hall table. There, he had taken care of everything.

The bedroom was full of personal touches all right. It was so personal, it looked as if the Vosserts had just gotten up. Both beds were unmade, clothes lay all over the room and a set of hot curlers plugged in on top of the dresser was red hot. A good way to start a fire, Matt thought as he unplugged them.

He didn't know quite what to expect, so when he pulled open the bedside table drawer, the sight of the handgun caught him up short. He reached in to pick it up, then, thinking in terms of fingerprints, changed his mind. It was a .38 snub-nosed double action Smith & Wesson, with hand-carved walnut grips. With its two-inch long barrel, it was some powerful weapon. So Vossert had a gun. Actually, it was no big deal. Probably as many people in Phoenix carried handguns as they did in Denver.

Matt carefully pushed the gun aside with his finger so he could check out the two little blue books that lay under it. They were passports. Now he was getting somewhere. Quickly he flipped through Mrs. Vossert's book to her picture. But when he saw it, he groaned out loud. Mrs. Vossert #2's photograph stared back at him. Not the Mrs. Vossert he had first met. Not the Mrs. Vossert who had disappeared. It was the Mrs. Vossert who had been passing herself off as Sidney Hanna Vossert all these weeks. Although her blond hair showed dark roots and every line and wrinkle was visible so that she looked ten years older, there was no mistaking the face.

Somehow this passport had been faked. Everyone and everything was confirming that he was wrong, that Mrs. Vossert was Mrs. Vossert was Mrs. Vossert. But he wasn't wrong. He knew it and he'd prove it if he had to tear this house apart. As he threw the passports back in the drawer, something slipped out of one of them. It was an airline ticket. Mr. and Mrs. C.R. Vossert were booked one-way on

SwissAir flying to Geneva, Switzerland, this coming Friday. That meant in three days' time the Vosserts would be leaving East Tedham forever. But they couldn't. Once they were gone, it would be too late to prove anything.

In a frenzy of frustration, Matt started yanking open drawers, pawing through the contents, slamming them shut. He found nothing, absolutely nothing that he wouldn't find in anyone's dresser drawers, and the double closets were cluttered with racks of ordinary coats and clothes and shoes. Four suitcases were stacked against the back closet wall. Matt pulled them out. Two of the cases were tagged with Vossert's name and a Phoenix address, and two were tagged with Mrs. Vossert's name and the same Phoenix address. And they were all empty. With an expletive, Matt heaved them back in the closet and kicked the door shut after them. There wasn't one trace of the first Mrs. Vossert anywhere. That cool bastard had thought of everything.

Cool, the word cool was the key. Vossert had been cool all right, and cool was winning. If Matt didn't stay cool too, he'd obliterate himself the way he'd almost been obliterated last weekend.

Clenching his teeth as if that would help him simmer down, Matt reopened the closet, straightened the shoes and clothes and restacked the suitcases the way he had found them. Then he rearranged the dresser drawers and carefully placed the passports back under the gun. Reluctantly he closed the bedside table drawer. How he'd love to slip that gun in his pocket. No one, including Vossert, could obliterate him then.

Matt checked out the bathroom next. It was as untidy and as unproductive as the bedroom, with damp towels and jars and bottles of makeup, all over the place. The kitchen revealed even less. That left only one place to look, the loft off the living room. Matt had just started up the ladder into the loft when he heard it, a frantic tapping behind him. He whirled around, his heart tripping somewhere high up in his chest. This time he knew it was Julie, but he also sensed that this time her knocking was tinged with panic. He jumped off the ladder, ran to the sliding door and pulled back the drapery.

Julie's face was pressed against the glass, her eyes almost opaque with fear. "They're coming back." Her voice penetrated thinly through the heavy door.

But Vossert had said they would be gone all day. Maybe Julie was wrong. No, one look at her face and Matt knew she had seen them, all right. He had to get out of the house fast. But as soon as he opened the sliding door, Julie's hand against his chest pushed him back in.

"Get inside," she ordered. "Their car's already up the hill. There's no way to get off the deck without them seeing us."

She was right. And even if they could get off the deck, there was no place to hide. The salt marsh offered no protection at all, and there wasn't a good-sized tree anywhere on the property. Blast this flat, barren Cape Cod landscape anyway. But where could they hide in the house? By now the two of them were circling the living room in agitated little dance steps. The loft. They both thought of the loft at the same moment and almost knocked each other down in their rush for the ladder. Women and children in the lifeboats first, was all Matt could think of as he let Julie climb up the ladder ahead of him.

Wait, the sliding door was still open. Matt raced over and pulled the door shut. But his fingers wouldn't coordinate enough to lock it. He'd have to leave it and hope Vossert wouldn't notice. He tore back across the living room and up the ladder after Julie. One small window shone faint dusty light into the loft.

"Sst, I'm over here," Julie stage-whispered from somewhere by the far wall.

Thunk! It was the unmistakable closing of a car door

in the driveway below. Now Matt's heart skipped from his chest into his throat where it lodged like a giant chicken bone cutting off his air.

Click. That was the key in the front door lock. Be grateful for small favors. If the Vosserts had come in the back, they'd have found it open where Matt had left it unlocked.

Bang! The front door slammed.

Panting as if the short scramble up the ladder had used up all the reserve in his lungs, Matt slid one foot in front of the other, praying that the uneven floorboards wouldn't squeak or that he wouldn't bump into any of the clutter that filled the loft. He couldn't see Julie's face, but he could see her silhouette huddled in a corner, half hidden behind a pile of suitcases. Step by careful step, he inched his way over. As soon as he reached her, he crouched down too, pressing against her slender length. She was trembling. Or maybe it was he who was trembling. It didn't matter. They were in this together. Matt reached over and put his arm around her and with his other hand took both her hands in his.

22

The heat from the whole house seemed to be trapped under the eaves and Matt was dripping the way he had when he had a fever with the mono. A trickle of wetness crept down his face, but he didn't dare move to wipe it off. Immobilized, he just huddled beside Julie getting more and more light-headed as if the sweat were draining off all his strength.

With no insulation in the house, every sound echoed. Now Vossert's footfall entered the living room. Matt gripped Julie's hands so tight, her knuckles cracked. Surely Vossert must have heard the sound. Apparently not, for he kept on going past the loft ladder, through the living room and into the hall. He hesitated a moment in the hall, then continued on into the bedroom. Matt strained to hear a second set of footsteps, lighter, high-heeled footsteps, but there were none. Vossert was alone. Now his tread came out of the bedroom, back through the hall and past the loft ladder.

Bang! The front door slammed shut. Unbelievably, a few seconds later, the car door thumped shut too, and Matt heard the smooth Cadillac engine start up, back out the driveway and fade away down the hill. They were gone. Neither Matt nor Julie spoke or even looked at each other as they tried to assimilate their incredible good fortune.

"You're stepping on my foot." Julie was almost sobbing.

Matt knew how she felt. He was pretty choked up himself. "Sorry about that," he croaked back as he slid his cramped arm from behind Julie's shoulder and tried to stand up. But his left leg was asleep and he lurched forward against the pile of suitcases. Before he could catch himself, both he and the suitcases went over with a crash. Momentarily shaken, he untangled himself and righted the suitcases. That was strange. Not only did the suitcases look brand new, but they were also as heavy as if they were fully packed.

"Why do you think the Vosserts came back?" Julie pressed her face against the loft window trying to see down the street.

"I have no idea," Matt muttered as he dragged the suitcases over to the light. Although there were no tags on them, S.H.V. was clearly stamped on both suitcases as well as on the little overnight case. Matt had certainly seen a good deal of those initials lately.

"Do you think they're gone for good?" Julie still sounded worried.

By now Matt was totally absorbed in the suitcases and didn't answer. He sprang the latch and opened the largest one.

The suitcase was full, neatly packed with women's clothes, sweaters, blouses, nightgowns, shoes. Matt began to pull everything out, not haphazardly this time, but carefully, one item at a time. Mrs. Vossert must have packed all these things for her trip to Switzerland on Friday.

Now Julie was kneeling beside him. "What's all this stuff?"

"Check the other suitcase. And the little case too," Matt directed.

Julie opened both of them. "It's more clothes," she said. "Slacks, dresses, shoes, robes. The little case is nothing but makeup and a set of hot curlers. And look, a bottle of Mojeau perfume. It sells for $75 a half ounce." Julie opened the bottle and with a laugh splashed a dab behind either ear.

"Hot curlers and makeup?" Matt repeated. But there was a hot curler set downstairs and enough makeup and perfume to supply a female army. Not only that, but Mrs. Vossert's closet was already full to bursting with clothes and shoes. And suitcases. There were four empty suitcases in that same closet, two tagged Charles R. Vossert and two tagged Sidney H. Vossert.

Julie was sorting through the contents of the other suitcase. She held up a red knit dress against herself. The skirt landed somewhere between her hips and knees and the sleeves didn't reach much below her elbows. "Mrs. Vossert must be really small. And short."

But Mrs. Vossert wasn't small. Or short either. When Matt had stood next to her in the kitchen, she had been his height which was almost six feet tall. "Mrs. Vossert is taller than you and heavier too," he said.

"She couldn't be. These clothes wouldn't fit me if I shrank six inches and lost twenty pounds," Julie insisted.

Matt looked down at the open suitcase. Julie was right. These clothes would never fit Mrs. Vossert. But if they were packed in S.H.V.'s luggage and they weren't S.H.V.'s clothes, whose clothes were they?

Instant insight hit Matt and Julie simultaneously. Startled, they looked into each other's eyes and the impact of that exchange rocked Matt back on his heels. Neither of them spoke.

"So how tall was the first Mrs. Vossert?" Julie finally

asked. She was whispering again as if the question were too momentous to articulate out loud.

"I don't know, but I'd guess she was short," Matt whispered back, recalling how low she had sat in the car that first day, almost like a child.

"If she'd left her husband or gone on a trip, she'd have taken her bags. Her overnight case, anyway." Julie's eyes were wide.

Matt nodded. His mother had packed enough for her quick trip to Denver to last a month.

"What do you think has happened to her?" Julie spoke slowly as if she wasn't sure she wanted to hear the answer.

And Matt wasn't sure he wanted to give one. Gone, that's what had happened. Disappeared. Discarded. Her name and identity taken by someone else. It was almost as if she had never been. But she had. Matt had seen her and now he had proof.

Julie must have been thinking the same thoughts. She rubbed behind her ears where she'd dabbed the perfume, trying to erase it. "What do we do now?" Her voice was still low and frightened.

"Go to the police. Put everything back in the suitcases and we'll take them to Constable Hulse."

"What if Constable Hulse arrests us for breaking and entering? And robbery?" Julie couldn't stand it another minute. She pulled a pack of gum from her pocket and slipped a piece in her mouth.

Matt scarcely noticed. If he could get through everything that had happened in the past half hour, he could certainly get through Julie chewing gum. As for the police, he would have to get through that too. If they were arrested, they were arrested. Julie may have forgotten, but he hadn't even wanted her to get near the house, let alone come in it. Although that had been her decision, for once he skipped the I-told-you-so.

This time it was men to the lifeboats first and Matt was down the loft ladder ahead of Julie. She passed the suitcases down, then followed with the overnight case. As soon as she reached the bottom, Matt set the suitcases down and put his hands on her shoulders. Her face was smudged and dirty and a stringy cobweb stranded across her sweatshirt.

"Hey, Julie, we did it. You and me."

"Yeah, but next time let's not make it quite so hairy, okay?"

Matt had to admit his insides were still churning too. At least they had each other. Matt put his arms around Julie and buried his face in her hair. It smelled of shampoo and $75-a-half-ounce perfume and the sneezy dust of the loft. In return, Julie tilted her head back and gave him a shaky smile. Now her eyes were pale gray, the color of her sweatshirt. And then her eyelids closed and so did Matt's as they leaned toward each other and kissed. It was a kiss of companionship and reassurance and comforting, and it was nice. Julie pulled away first.

"Let's get going. This place freaks me out."

Carrying the overnight case, Julie led the way, through the kitchen and out the back door, with Matt struggling awkwardly behind with the two heavy bags bumping against his legs. They were already beyond Bluff Cottage property when Matt suddenly stopped.

"Wait for me in the Land Rover, Julie. I'll be right back," he called.

Without waiting for her response, Matt shoved the suitcases under a nearby juniper shrub and ran back to the house. He was so pleased with himself he was whistling under his breath as he unlocked the back door and dashed through the kitchen into the bedroom. Grabbing a clean tissue, he carefully picked up a jar of Mrs. Vossert's night cream from the dresser and slipped it in his down vest pocket. It was bound to have her fingerprints all over it and for sure they wouldn't match the fingerprints on the contents of the suitcases he and Julie had found in the loft. Now all the parts of the puzzle were neatly fitted in place to present to Constable Hulse.

But as Matt headed back into the kitchen, his whistle faded to a wheeze. Charles Vossert was leaning against the back kitchen door, blocking it. More than blocking it, consuming that whole end of the room with his broad bulk. Matt's body seemed to go limp as bright bursts of terror exploded in his head. All he could think of as he stared at Vossert's dark, glittery eyes and narrow hook nose was that raptor marsh hawk swooping down on a helpless victim, its talons outstretched.

23

Nothing occurred to Matt, not an alibi, not flight, not even fear. He had seen animals freeze into a kind of acquiescence just before that marsh hawk struck and that was what happened to him now. All he could do was try to hold his limbless body together and wait. Vossert unfolded his arms and smiled a tight smile.

"You seem to have a real problem, sonny."

Vossert's words were innocuous enough, but the cutting edge under them was as deliberate as a knife. Dully, Matt nodded agreement.

"What gives with you, anyway? You got some grudge against me?" The knife was probing.

This time Matt's head swung back and forth in a negative. No.

"You think you can break into my house without my knowing it?" Vossert's laugh sounded more like a bark. "As a matter of fact, you might have pulled it off if I hadn't come back to unplug those damned curlers and found that real estate card on the table." Vossert sounded surprised, almost impressed, as he pulled the Dobbins card from his pocket.

The hot curlers, that was why he came back, Matt thought irrelevantly as Vossert continued, "Once we were on the road again, I got to thinking. We'd only been gone twenty minutes, and in that time a real estate agent had already showed the house, plus thoughtfully unplugged those curlers? Not very likely. So I called Dobbins and they told me they don't even list this house, let alone show it. What do you say about that?"

"I say it was a good idea." Incredibly, those words had come from Matt, although he had certainly made no conscious decision to say them.

Vossert's half smile immediately vanished. "Good idea? Suppose we see what the police have to say about your good idea." In one quick motion, he had crossed the room and seized Matt's arm. Matt had gotten an electrical shock once and Vossert's touch galvanized him the same way now. A current of anger slammed through him and he jerked his arm away.

"You just do that. You call the police. That's fine with me." Matt shouted his defiance.

Immediately Vossert's smooth expression hardened into a tight knot and a quick fear flashed in his eyes.

That flash told Matt everything. It told him what a critical error he had made. It told him that Vossert had been fishing to find out how much Matt knew and now Vossert realized that Matt was more than a nuisance. He was a real threat. Above all, it told Matt that Vossert had killed his wife. What had been speculation before now became a reality and it was an unspoken fact between them. In that instant, such a surge of tension filled the room it expanded and pushed out the walls with its force.

Instead of riding with the waves and letting Vossert call the police, Matt had allowed his anger to plunge him in over his head. And he was too committed now to talk his way out with words. Retreat was the only option open to him. That sliding glass door in the living room. It must still be open where he hadn't been able to lock it.

Spinning around, Matt broke and ran into the hall and across the living room. He pushed back the draperies and shoved at the sliding door. It glided open and he was outside.

Incredibly, no footsteps pounded behind him. No shouts cried out. No hand struck down on his shoulder. Then Matt was swinging his feet over the edge of the deck as he grasped the railing and let himself down the twelve feet to the ground. He hit hard, turning his ankle under him. A sharp pain ran up his leg, but he couldn't stop now. He had to get back to the Land Rover. And safety.

"Stop! I have a gun."

Gun. The word vibrated in Matt's head. It was the gun in the bedroom. Vossert hadn't come after Matt because he had gone for his gun. Matt stopped so abruptly, pain grabbed his ankle like hot pincers.

And when he turned around, he saw Vossert on the deck in the exact spot where Julie had stood guard, out of sight from the road. He was holding the .38 Smith & Wesson and it was pointed right at Matt. Matt had instant tunnel vision so that all he could see was that gun, metallic, efficient, lethal. In all the years he had lived around guns, he had never had one pointed at him. It was terrifying. More than terrifying, traumatizing. All he could think of were those suitcases in the loft and how fragile the life had been that had packed them. That life was gone, wiped out, and now Matt was in the same position with no more guarantees than Sidney Vossert had been given. At the realization, dread seemed to weigh his whole body down. His head felt too heavy for his neck and his arms dangled leadenly at his sides.

Now Vossert was swinging down from the deck with far more agility than Matt had. As Vossert headed across the backyard, the gun still at the alert, he straightened his jacket. For some stupid reason, it occurred to Matt that Vossert was dressed for business, not a preposterous game of hide and seek. He wore a brown suit with fine blue lines through it. A blue necktie just matched the stripes and his suit just matched his eyes. His hair was wavy and dark, except for distinguished gray sideburns. He looked urbane. Substantial. Important. His appearance made the gun in his hand seem ludicrous.

"I left Sidney back in a Tedham coffee shop." Vossert's tone, businesslike too, implied that he was in a hurry and didn't want to prolong this nonsense. And he was all-business as he glanced at the house behind him, then east toward the ocean, then finally south over Matt's shoulder at the salt marsh. And all the time there was that gun.

"The marsh . . . you walk your dog in the marsh . . . across the sluice bridge to the beach . . ."

Matt automatically turned toward the marsh and looked at it, really looked. The nor'easter had devastated the whole area. What marsh grass wasn't underwater was flattened level. Bottles, cans, plastic containers, driftwood, all sorts of garbage that had washed through the sluice littered the landscape. The tide was coming in, with the water already up over the creek banks so that most of the smaller islands were underwater. There wasn't a sign of a bird or an animal anywhere.

"We're going down to the sluice." Vossert was trying to keep his voice even, but Matt sensed a tautness under his calm that warned Matt he should be on his guard, that he should be thinking ahead. *If Vossert does this, then I should do that. Or, if Vossert goes this way, then I should go that way.* But Matt wasn't planning anything at all. As the two of them walked toward the sluice, all he could think about was the fierce pain in his ankle.

And then they had reached the eight-foot-wide bridge over the sluice. The combination of the spring tides and the three-day storm had almost demolished it, tearing out some of the floorboards and ripping away the railing completely. How long it would last was anyone's guess. Even now the water rushed over the sluice dam only ten inches or so beneath the bridge floor, and cold spray shot up through the broken floorboards as the water, flowing from the ocean, merged in a single monstrous flume that thundered over the dam and into the marsh beyond in a crashing waterfall.

For some inane reason, Matt remembered a quote from *Macbeth* that they had been reading in English: ". . . a tale told by an idiot, full of sound and fury, signifying nothing." Only Matt knew this sound and fury signified plenty. One thing for sure, there was no question as to who the idiot was.

A hard nudge of the gun at Matt's back prodded him on and he knew it was an order to walk out on the bridge. Instinctively, he pulled his arms in tight against his sides, and as he did, he felt a hard lump in his vest pocket. It was the jar of face cream that he had lifted from the Vosserts' bedroom. Slowly he slipped his right hand into his pocket and gripped it tight.

Again Matt felt the nudge of the gun. The bridge was only twelve feet long, but it loomed like an endless pirate plank as he took a tentative step out onto it. Another step. But now the steely pressure was no longer in his back. He sensed, rather than saw, a sweeping motion behind him and he spun around. Vossert's arm was upraised, about to come down on him with the butt of the gun. In that fraction of a second, Matt ducked to his right and raised his left arm to ward off the blow. The gun smashed down on his forearm with bone-crushing force. Even as he cried out, he yanked the jar from his pocket with his other hand and slammed it down on Vossert's wrist. With a yelp of pain, Vossert dropped the gun and it clattered to the bridge floor. He dove to retrieve it, but it spun across the wet boards and disappeared over the edge into the water.

In that instant, everything changed. Matt was taller than Vossert, but Vossert was heavier and stronger. Even the business suit couldn't disguise his thick chest and the power of his shoulders. But Matt no longer felt any pain, not in his ankle, not in his arm. He was all concentration as he and Vossert faced each other, crouching, maneuvering on the narrow bridge. Vossert moved first, lunging at Matt with his arms outstretched. Matt sidestepped, but as he did, his feet slipped out from under him on the wet bridge floor. He fell hard on his back, and all the wind exploded out of him. He struggled to get up, but Vossert was already on top of him. Vossert's face purpled and the veins in his neck bulged as his big hands reached for Matt's throat.

The jar. Matt still had it. Gripping it tight with his numb fingers, he stiff-armed the jar in an arc and caught Vossert across the temple with a crack like a hardball hitting a mitt. His hand vibrated from the impact as Vossert's expression slackened, his body sagged, and he slumped to the bridge floor. As Vossert continued his slide toward the edge, he reached out, and from some deep reservoir of strength seized Matt's arm. It was a death grip and there was no releasing it. Matt flailed out with his other hand to hold onto something, anything, that would keep him from going over. But his fingers raked helplessly across the rough floorboards as Vossert's incredible strength pulled him to the edge. Falling seemed to take a slow-motion eternity, but it was only an instant in time before Vossert and Matt were over the side together.

24

Matt's immediate reaction to the water was *cold*, then slam, he smashed up against something solid. It was the sluice dam under the bridge. He and Vossert had fallen off the east side of the bridge where the water funneled in from the ocean. The tremendous force of the incoming tide had swept Matt under the bridge and slapped him up against the dam.

With only his head above water, Matt could see there was less than a foot of space between the water and the underside of the bridge. It was dark and the roar of the water confused him as he tried to get his bearings. But something underwater was bumping against his legs. It was heavy and solid, yet resilient too. Like a body. Vossert. It had to be Vossert. If Matt was pinned here against the dam wall, then Vossert would be too. But Vossert was hurt, maybe unconscious.

Now Vossert's inert body was sliding slowly across Matt's legs. In a moment, he would be out of reach. Matt filled his lungs with air, then hand over hand worked his way down through the icy water until he felt Vossert's broad back. He hooked his hand under Vossert's belt and kicked hard. As soon as their heads broke water, Matt shored Vossert up against the dam so that his head was above water.

Now to find a way out of here, and fast. If the freezing water didn't finish them off here in the darkness, then the incoming tide would. Full high tide would raise the water up to, and probably above, the level of the bridge, wiping out their air space.

Certainly they couldn't turn around and swim out. The force of the water at their backs had Matt and Vossert plastered up against the dam like wallpaper, and there was no way they could swim against it. The bridge overhead looked more promising. The cross beams were so close Matt could reach up and touch them. The last couple of high tides had ripped out a lot of the floorboards, which meant that the rest of the boards were probably loose too. If Matt could make an opening big enough to fit through, he could hike himself up onto the bridge and pull Vossert up after him.

Matt pounded his fist on a couple of the planks directly overhead. They rattled and shook but held fast. He tried again. Still he couldn't budge them. He sank back into the water, spent with exhaustion and cold. Icy salt water was flowing through his veins instead of blood.

But he couldn't give up. There was one last chance. He and Vossert could let themselves be carried by the flume of water over the dam and into the marsh beyond. Though it would mean only about an eight-foot ride, the top of the dam was all rotting timbers and jagged edges. And with less than a foot to spare between the water and the underside of the bridge, their heads would be terrifyingly close to the overhead cross beams. Even if they made it safely through the dam, they still had to survive the waterfall as it thundered into the marsh. But the marsh meant safety. Once over the waterfall, the force of the water eddied and swirled, then gradually dissipated into the familiar placid tidal creeks that looped through the marsh.

Risk or not, Matt knew they had to try it and every minute wasted was raising the water level under the bridge. And Vossert was a big, barrel-chested man who would need every inch of headroom he could get. He'd have to go first so Matt could line him up in position to shoot the flume. But Vossert was a problem. He was only semiconscious now, and if he didn't make it through, he'd be like a cork stopping up the whole space so Matt wouldn't be able to get past him.

Matt's heartbeat swelled to fill his whole chest. He had to get out of here. He couldn't stand the cold, the dark, the roaring pressure at his back another minute. He'd shoot the flume first and leave Vossert to get out on his own. Matt certainly didn't owe him anything. He had tried to kill Matt, hadn't he? Matt glanced at Vossert. His hair was flattened wetly to his head and water was running down his gray face. There was a lump by his eye where Matt had hit him, but no blood. The water had probably frozen his blood like it had Matt's.

Vossert must have sensed Matt studying him. He groaned, turned and opened his eyes. They were clear and comprehending as if he knew what Matt was considering. Matt could only stare back. And then Vossert reached up and rubbed his ear as if it hurt him. Matt swallowed past the rawness of his throat. His ears ached the same way. That connection wiped out any thought of leaving Vossert behind. To hurt was to be human. No matter what that person had done, for this present moment, that person was alive and that was enough.

Matt heaved Vossert up by the seat of his pants and grabbed hold of his feet to give him the final push over. Vossert's feet were bare. The force of the water must have torn off his shoes and socks. Matt wiggled his own feet to check if they were bare too, but they were frozen stumps at the ends of his legs. It didn't matter. He had to get Vossert started.

"Keep your head down. Put your arms out," Matt shouted. Although the rush of the water tore away his words, Vossert nodded weakly. Now he was up and over the top of the dam.

Swoosh. Vossert was swept away from Matt's hands as helpless as a piece of balsa wood, with only inches between him and the underside of the bridge. Head down. Let the water do the work. There, Vossert was almost through. Then it happened. His back thumped up against the underside of the bridge and his body bucked to the left from the impact. The whole length of him twisted awkwardly and jerked to a stop as his foot caught on something. Now he was sprawled diagonally across the dam with the water surging around him.

Matt didn't give himself time to breathe, think, decide. He just hoisted himself up onto the dam, stretched out his arms and shot off into the chute of water. Immediately he was jammed up against Vossert, with the deafening turbulence of the water enveloping both of them. With his last bit of working strength, he grabbed Vossert's foot from where it was wedged and yanked it. The foot released with a burst of Vossert's bright blood. Now the momentum of the current picked Vossert up and flung him though the rest of the flume with Matt catapulted along behind him.

The headlong ride snatched Matt's breath away as he was suddenly launched into the air like a blast from a cannon. He soared straight out, coming down hard in a belly flop. Instantly he was sucked into the water, devoured, boiled, tossed. There was no fighting or trying to get out of it. All he could do was curl up and tuck his head on his chest. Little by little, the sucking power of the water began to lessen. Don't fight it. Relax. Mrs. Shreve's words circled in his head and he forced himself to let his arms and legs dangle. Not knowing which way was up, he didn't dare kick or swim in any direction. Then, almost imperceptibly, he sensed himself moving upward and his head surfaced.

"Matt." From some distant place he heard his name. "Matt."

He didn't have the strength to answer.

"I'm here, Matt. It's okay." That voice again.

Now there was a furious splashing from nearby. Some-one was swimming toward him. Julie. That had been Julie's voice and now Julie was reaching out her arms to support him. Her long wet hair was swept behind her ears and Matt saw she had big ears just like his. For some crazy reason, he had an urge to laugh, but his whole body, including his face, was frozen into paralysis.

"Hold on," Julie gasped. As she started pulling him toward shore, all he could hear was the in-and-out of her breathing and the roar of the waterfall behind them.

Then Julie was dragging him up on the bank and over the sharp marsh grass. Someone else was already lying on the creek bank. It was Vossert, facedown with his legs and bare feet trailing in the water. Julie must have pulled him out too. He was so still, Matt couldn't tell if he was dead or alive. But he had to be alive. Matt had risked everything to save him.

Julie collapsed shivering on the grass between them. "Oh, Matt, I thought you were gone . . . I didn't see you . . ." she hiccuped as she tried to catch her breath. "The police, I called them . . . they're coming." Her words broke off in a sob and sudden tears merged with the water streaming from her hair.

Matt wanted to reassure her, had to reassure her, but he was too numb and weak to formulate anything as com-plicated as a reassurance. All he was able to do was reach over and press her hand. She pressed his in return and for the moment, it was enough for both of them.

25

Matt opened the pickup door for Julie. "Old Man Pettingill would kill me if he knew I was giving you a ride." It was true. Mr. Pettingill had made it clear from the start. No passengers.

Julie laughed as she threw her books on the pickup floor and climbed in. "With what Mom spends at Pettingill's every month, he can afford to give me a ride."

Julie had had a 2:30 dentist's appointment in town and Matt had arranged to pick her up when she was finished. So far he'd already been waiting twenty minutes.

"I've got a couple of stops in East Tedham, then I'll drop you off at your house." He shifted gears and headed out Schoolhouse Lane. "Mrs. Shreve is my first delivery."

"She's out of the hospital?"

"Yeah, she got out this morning and her daughter Donna phoned in a grocery order."

"I'll wait here," Julie offered as Matt pulled into Mrs. Shreve's driveway. Before he was even out of the pickup, she'd managed to get a piece of gum in her mouth. Half an hour in the dentist's chair must be as long as she could go without gum.

Donna opened the back door. "Hi, Matt, come on in."

He carried in the groceries and set them on the kitchen table.

"Why don't you go in and say hello to Mother, Matt. But please don't stay too long." Donna started to put away the groceries.

Mrs. Shreve was seated in her usual chair by the wood stove. Her leg, still in its cast, was propped up on a footstool.

"Hi, Mrs. Shreve."

"Matt, it's so good to see you." She held out her hand and when Matt took it, it seemed perfectly natural to lean down and kiss her. Her skin was dry and powdery cool. She was still pale, but her eyes were bright.

"First of all, tell me about Bucky." As Mrs. Shreve tucked her afghan around her, Matt noticed how gnarled and thin her hands were, all ridged with blue veins.

"Mom and Bucky got home the day before yesterday. Mom was awarded custody of Bucky which means Bucky will live with us and spend his summers in Colorado." Bucky and his mother had returned two days after Matt's little misadventure. The Vossert thing had almost overshadowed the excitement about Bucky. Almost, but not quite.

"That's wonderful, Matt. And for pity's sake, I've certainly been reading all about you." Mrs. Shreve pointed to the *Cape Cod Tribune* spread out on the table.

Matt should have felt triumphant. After all, he had been right and if he hadn't persisted, Vossert and that woman would have long since been safe in Switzerland. But he didn't feel triumphant. All he felt was tired, tired of police questions, tired of the publicity, tired of everyone pumping him. He didn't even want to hash it over with

Mrs. Shreve, but he could see by her expression that she was dying to hear only was too polite to ask.

"Well, most of it's in the paper, I guess. Mrs. Vossert's family owned Hanna Industries, some big company out in Phoenix that was sold so that Mrs. Vossert came into a lot of money and stocks and securities. Vossert had power of attorney for her which meant he could cash in on every-thing she owned. He got her to come here for a rest on Cape Cod where no one knew them, then almost as soon as they arrived, he killed her and had his girl friend take her place. He and the girl friend were on their way to Boston to pick up the money from the sale of Mrs. Vossert's stocks and securities the day Julie and I fouled them up."

Only Matt knew how close he had come to messing up the whole thing. If he had let Vossert call the police the way he wanted to instead of losing his temper, he wouldn't have risked everything, including both Vossert's life and his own. As it was, blowing his cool had him limping around with a sprained ankle and a sore arm from where Vossert had hit him with the gun butt. Still, to be fair to himself, there were encouraging signs that he was occa-sionally capable of riding with the waves instead of forever fighting against them.

Mrs. Shreve shook her head. "Staid old East Tedham can scarce comprehend such goings-on."

"Actually Constable Hulse remembered what I had said about Mrs. Vossert's hand and had already ordered a computer check on her." Matt swallowed. "It was through the computer check that they were able to identify the real Mrs. Vossert's . . . the . . . her body." Incredibly, Vos-sert had driven the body to the other side of Cape Cod, released the brake on his car and let the car, body and all sink in Dawkins Swamp. Then, cool operator that he was, he'd gone out and bought an identical gray Cadillac.

"At least Lemuel Hulse had the common sense to . . ."

153

Honk-a-honk.

It was the pickup horn. Matt had forgotten all about Julie waiting outside. "I gotta go, Mrs. Shreve. I'll bring Tebby back tonight." A stab of regret pierced him at the thought.

Mrs. Shreve held up her hand. "I'm really not able to care for Tebby any more, Matt. Is there a chance you could keep her permanently?"

A chance? There certainly was. Bucky was crazy about Tebby and even Mom admitted she had missed having a dog around. "I'll say I can. I mean, I know you hate to give her up but we'd love to have her." Matt pictured Tebby's soft golden-brown eyes and seal-sleek coat. Tebby. His.

"Good." Mrs. Shreve smiled and closed her eyes.

"Good-bye, Mrs. Shreve," Matt said softly. He left by the front door, closing it quietly behind him.

"I thought you were going to deliver their groceries, not cook and serve their dinner." Julie was definitely irritated.

Matt made an effort to ignore her annoyance. "Mrs. Shreve is giving me Tebby. Isn't that great? We haven't had a dog since Sarge died." He backed out the driveway and turned onto Uncle Clement's Road.

"Hey, that's all right." Julie could recoup too, and she sounded pleased for him. As they reached the crest of the hill, Julie turned and looked out her window. "Look, Bluff Cottage is all boarded up. Have you heard how Vossert's doing?"

Matt shruggged. "He's still in the hospital under guard. His head's okay, but his foot got mangled up going through the sluice. Constable Hulse says he and the woman will probably be indicted by a grand jury and stand trial." And Matt and Julie would have to be witnesses. He hadn't even wanted Julie to get involved and now she had to testify. What was worse, both of them had to answer charges for breaking and entering, just like Julie had predicted. But as state witnesses, Constable Hulse practically guaranteed they'd get off with nothing more than a slap on the wrist.

Matt looked over at Julie as he pulled into the first house on Windjammer Way for a delivery. It was his good luck that Julie had gotten involved. Where would he be now if she hadn't? He opened his door, but didn't get out.

"I . . . I guess I never thanked you for being there to pull me out of the water, Julie. I was in bad shape . . . and might not have made it . . ." He hadn't blushed for three years and here he was, turning crimson.

Julie studied her hands, embarrassed too. "You'd have made it okay, Matt. I just gave you a little help."

As Matt lifted the carton from the back of the pickup, he decided "a little help" was an understatement. Julie had waited in the Land Rover, then when he hadn't returned, came looking for him. That was when she had seen Vossert walk him down to the sluice at gunpoint. Julie had waited until he and Vossert were out of sight, then she'd sneaked into Bluff Cottage and called the police from there. She'd made it back down to the marsh just in time to see both Matt and Vossert go over the side of the bridge.

When Matt climbed back in the pickup after making his delivery, neither he nor Julie mentioned their moment of awkwardness. They drove in silence as Matt hooked a right back onto Uncle Clement's Road and headed down the hill past Nimicut Salt Marsh.

"Matt, stop!" Julie cried.

Matt braked hard, and almost before they had stopped, Julie was out of the pickup and running toward the path that led into the marsh. Not about to be left behind, Matt jumped out too, trying not to put too much weight on his bad ankle as he followed her.

By the time he caught up to her, she had reached

Black Rock. It was dead low tide, and now, a week after the nor'easter, there were already signs of recovery. With most of the debris and litter swept out to sea by the tides, the marsh grass looked greener and healthier. It was a washed-clean soft April day with the distant ocean glittering a million miles in every direction.

"Look, Matt." Julie pointed across the marsh.

It was the fox. He was trotting along one of the creek banks as bold as could be, holding a catch in his mouth that looked like a mouse or a small bird. And there ahead of him on the bank were two small fox pups. Matt sucked in his breath when he saw them and Julie gasped too.

The dark-furred pups were roughhousing. The larger of the two jumped in the air and pounced on the other one, knocking them both over. Now the smaller one lay on his back and kicked his thin legs in the air while the larger pup nipped at him playfully. They seemed oblivious to everything until their father approached. Immediately they got up on awkward little legs and followed him across a creek bed out of sight into the tall grass.

POW! Matt remembered how he had once taken imaginary aim at that male fox. Killing him would be simple. Matt had never killed an animal, but he had certainly seen how easy it was to do. Vossert could have killed Matt easily too. When his gun had been dredged out of the marsh, it had six hollow point bullets in it, any one of which would have blasted Matt to kingdom come. All of a sudden, just the thought of pulling the trigger on that fox turned Matt's stomach. His pulling the trigger on another creature would mean a judgment on his part that some other life was less important than his own had been at the moment Vossert had leveled that gun at him. Killing the fox or any other animal was no longer possible for Matt. Not ever.

"Oh, Matt, isn't that fox family beautiful?" In her excitement, Julie threw her arms around Matt.

"Yeah." Enjoying the hug, Matt returned it with gusto.

"I'm going to try and get the Muir Club kids down here tomorrow to observe them. I'll start up our phone relay to let everyone know . . ." Julie chattered on but Matt only half listened.

He'd come too. He'd bring his camera and take pictures. If any of them turned out, maybe the school newspaper would run them. He glanced over at Julie who was still talking.

"Hey, I gotta go," she interrupted herself. "Mom's waiting to go shopping with me."

Matt would have liked to stay longer. He could have spent the whole afternoon with Julie, but he had to get going too.

"Yeah, and if I don't finish my deliveries, Pettingill will give me the ax," he said only half jokingly. He grabbed Julie's hand and the two of them hurried along the marsh path back to the pickup.

As soon as they were out of sight, a flock of red-winged blackbirds alighted on the swaying reeds calling to one another in liquid song. The great blue heron drifted down from a nearby perch to silently stalk the low tidal banks and the marsh hawk glided low over the meandering creeks before taking off into the sky with a beat of its strong wings, soaring, soaring.